The Accidental HAREM

By JJ Knight

FIRST EDITION
ISBN: 978-1985782587

Also by JJ Knight

The UNCAGED LOVE Series
The FIGHT FOR HER Series
SINGLE DAD ON TOP
SINGLE DAD PLUS ONE

www.jjknight.com

For all the girls who do their own thing

1: Vivienne

I never have been very traditional.

Case in point number one: I started coloring my hair strawberry blond when I was sixteen.

Mother didn't know. She'd have skinned me alive. I was very tricky about it, pretending to have a hat fetish. She didn't see my full head of hair for almost a year, when I was a senior and she couldn't do diddly squat to punish me as I had already been accepted to junior college.

Daddy said he liked it anyway, and he's the one who always handed over the car keys. What does it matter what color your hair is anyway? Gramma always says it's what inside that matters. And I am loyal and kind and have zero problems with anybody's way of living. Gramma taught me all that too, even when we sometimes felt full-on surrounded by jerks and cheats.

But strawberry blond is my *color*. The darker kind. I'm too lazy for platinum. We are L'Oreal soulmates. Till death do I part from my squeezy chemical bottle.

Case in point number two: I slept with my first boyfriend at age fifteen.

Okay, I know. You think I was too young. You'd probably be right. But boys were just so…how do I explain it? More than interesting. More than fun. Intoxicating. *Necessary*.

I became a serial monogamist right off. I learned never to jump one ship until another was in the harbor. So I never cheated, no way. But there *might* have been a rather narrow window in between them every once in a while.

I like to be passionate, both in bed and at the microphone.

Case in point number three: I want to be a country music singer.

I'm aware that I'd probably get more fame as a pop star. But country music is in my bones, growing up in Tennessee. Love gone wrong. Oh that "Lonesome Me." "Tear in My Beer." I like the songs with a powerful gut punch.

"He Stopped Loving Her Today" makes me cry for an hour every single dang time. Yeah. Google it.

It's a tear jerker in the hands of George Jones. I've also heard Dolly do it. LeeAnn did it. All good.

I may or may not have recorded a version for YouTube.

Despite my aspirations, I'm twenty-five and work as a travel agent. It's a good gig, as I more or less set my hours, work on commission, and can use my travel discounts to go to auditions, which isn't easy since I live in Miami now.

Plus I get big perks on cruises, and I always choose the ones for singles. Everybody hooks up in every direction there, and nobody blinks an eye when we don't even exchange last names.

Karaoke is standard fare on these ships, and I know if I can get up there and sing a soulful rendition of "Crazy," I'm going to have my choice of men that night. Works every time.

Does this make me a tramp? Maybe. I don't know. I like to think of it as sexual agency. Boys have always been able to sow their oats.

I just planted a couple of fields of my own.

All this is to say is that when hunkalicious in jeans and cowboy boots walks into our office to book a cruise, I am all over it. My coworker Sam, who just finished her transition to the Sam she was meant to be, sees him saunter in and instantly waves him over

3

to me. Sam likes girls regardless of her gender. We can generally eyeball which direction to send a walk-in within three steps of the door.

We refer the retired couples back to Janet. She loves helping them find bargain tours with the least amount of walking. Sam and I are hopeless at those.

We're all about the adventure, the perfect pairing of the dream vacation with the ideal package.

And I'm already eying this guy's package.

I cut him a shy smile. Sam may have sent him to me, but I did see her check out his Wranglers. She might like girls, but she's got eyes.

And that butt is *gold*.

I stand up and hold out a hand, tilting my head so a dangling earring will peep out from my hair. I've practiced this look in the mirror. I want to dazzle the man I'm interested in. There is no room to be coy. Nothing about me translates as *hard to get*.

Case in point number four: I'm easy.

But you've figured that out by now. Hopefully you're not judging me. Because by the time this story is done, I'll have done a lot more than just sing a few songs and bang a few boys.

But back to the hunk.

He drops into the chair. His smile is slow and full of more promise than a TV talent show. Which I've auditioned for, three times. Those lips would have made a drag queen cry. You could kiss every part of them for the better part of an hour and not cover all the territory.

Despite being ready to take him on my lunch break, and dinner, and *breakfast*, I manage to sit up straight and ask him what sort of trip he's thinking about. All the while imagining how that sandy brown hair would feel running through my fingertips.

I get another slow smile. God, I need an air conditioner in January. Of course, here on the ocean I'd need one anyway. But you get my drift. The back of my neck is as hot as the back of his jeans.

"The Blue Sapphire Yacht site says you're an authorized agency," he says, and his voice is just as sexy as his lips. Low, rumbly, like a tractor in a field.

I'm already naked in the hay with him while he mentions that Blue Sapphire Yachts was hard to track down. Their online presence is a little short on information.

And with reason. Their cruises start at ten thousand dollars.

Per day.

I size him up. Dusty boots. Wranglers. Totally need to peruse *those* again. A half-buttoned blue checked flannel over a white T-shirt. Nice hair, but not anything high-end in cut or style.

No watch. The phone sticking out of his pocket is a run-of-the-mill iPhone, the previous version, not the newest.

He looks pretty normal. Although he definitely works out. That means he has a job that encourages it or else he has leisure time. Access to a gym or equipment at home.

Still, I'm not seeing $50,000 cruise material. And that's the starter package.

"They are pricey," I say. I tug out a brochure for a more reasonable option. "Any particular reason why you chose them? You can get really nice cruises for much less." I open the tri-fold to show a lovely ship on a deep blue sea.

It's a singles cruise. One I'm thinking of taking in a couple months.

I'm shameless.

But he dashes my hopes.

"No, I'm pretty specific," he says. "I need the Blue Sapphire Yacht Cruise starting three weeks from now sailing from Miami to Cuba."

"Okay," I say. The brochure goes back in the rack, and I turn to my computer. "Let me see what their schedule is. Three weeks out isn't long. It might be booked."

He nods, a flash of doubt crossing his handsome face. I'm not opposed to sitting here with him across the desk a little longer, even if I seriously doubt he can afford a Blue Sapphire Yacht. I'll have to figure out a way to present the figure to him without embarrassing him when he realizes how far off the mark he is.

Of course, who knows. Maybe he won a lottery. Or inherited some cash. And it's not unheard of for people to live way below their means or to hide their wealth.

It's just that rich people don't come in person to book a Blue Sapphire. They have assistants or secretaries do that.

And newly rich people wouldn't have heard of them. Even as an authorized agency, we're not allowed to mention them unless the customer talks about them first.

Blue Sapphire Yachts doesn't advertise. There's no way to know unless you just…know. When someone takes you on one. Or a company sends you there. It's a secret passed by word of mouth. Like a kiss.

A hot kiss on a pair of lips made for sinnin'.

"You okay?" the man asks.

Damn, I'm staring.

"Just waiting for the numbers to crunch," I say,

swinging back to my screen. Of course the numbers crunched instantaneously, but people are always blaming their slowness on their computers. I do it at least twice a day.

I scan the screen. There are six Blue Sapphire Yacht cruises involving Cuba in the next month.

"I've found several," I say. "Was it five days? Seven? Ten?"

He frowns. "I'm not sure. I heard them mention Grand Cayman."

I wonder who "them" are. Maybe he's going with friends as hot as himself. I imagine being surrounded by Wranglers and several of his hot buddies, and my face flushes.

"That helps," I manage to say. The five-day boat doesn't stop in Grand Cayman. It has to be either the seven-day one or the ten. I hit print on both.

"I've found two," I tell him. I lean down to pull the print outs from the tray below. His eyes go where I'm hoping they will, into the cleavage that pops as I bend.

I'm sooo glad I wore the wrap around dress today. It fits like a dream, and I can conceal or reveal as I choose.

This guy warrants a reveal.

"How did you hear about Blue Sapphire Yachts?"

I ask as I lay the printouts on the table. "They don't advertise."

His gaze skitters down my body and onto the papers. "I have a business connection taking this one. He suggested I look into it."

"Oh." So maybe he is all right. This is a corporate expense. Except nothing about Wranglers says *business*. Unless he's getting up in *my* business.

"Well, here are the two in that time frame." I turn the pages around. "Blue Sapphire Yachts are very exclusive. This one is mostly booked, but it looks like I can get you on." I point to the seven-day cruise.

"This one is oddly open." I turn it back around. "This itinerary was just created a few days ago."

"That's it," he says quickly. "That's the one. I want on it."

My eyebrows lift. I can see Sam watching us, probably now regretting sending Wranglers to me. The commission on this one cruise is what I make in a week. Two weeks, when it's slow.

I circle the price in my pen. "This work, though?" It's six figures. Low six figures, but still, six.

He hesitates. "Can I put a down payment on it and pay the rest in a week?"

"Sure," I say. "But if you don't cover it, you forfeit the down payment."

He nods slowly. "I'll have it. I have money coming."

I was right about not being easy rich. But now he's got me curious. I glance at Sam, who quickly turns like she wasn't listening in.

I lean forward. "You sure? I can get you lots of nice places for less."

His eyes drop to the V of my neckline and rest there a moment. I haven't even displayed this angle on purpose. But he seems to be enjoying the view, so I keep it there. My boobs are one of the few parts of my body I'm not shy about. Hell, I'm not *shy* about anything, but maybe self-conscious is the word. I only like my belly when I'm lying flat on my back.

And my thighs are hopeless.

But back to Wranglers.

"No, this is the one," he says. He has to wrestle his eyes back to my face. "You book many of these cruises?"

I shrug, and the movement drags his attention back to my cleavage. "There are only three authorized Blue Sapphire agencies in Miami," I say. "The company has very particular requirements."

His eyes come back to mine now, inquisitive. "And what are those?"

"I'll have to fill out a background screen on you,"

I say. "And take a photo and go over some of their policies. We're trained special for them."

Now his smile is lazy. "When do you take my picture and ask me questions?"

He's flirting.

Okay, my lady bits are starting to sizzle. "I'm sure a gentleman traveler such as yourself has a favorite restaurant?"

Yes, friends, I just invited myself on a date.

I do this often.

He sits back, scrutinizing me. "Is there a high rate of denial on this screening?" he asks.

And I get it. He's playing me too. He thinks I can get him in. But I'm super crazy curious, and he's the hottest one-night stand I've spotted in a while. So I'll go along.

"The price is a pretty high barrier already," I say. "But I'm sure there are some unsavory ways of earning money that they prefer to screen out. The boats are small, and the clients are interested in protection and privacy."

He relaxes a bit. "That makes sense, actually. So I suppose I should pick you up for this interrogation after work?"

Now I'm smiling. "I get off at six," I say. It's four actually, but I want to run home and prep a little for this one. Some waxing. Some spritzing.

He stands. "Then I'll return at six."

I hop up from my chair, aware that my boobs get a good sway on as I do. "I'm Vivienne Carter," I say. "And you are?" I hold out my hand.

He extends a strong hand and accepts mine. "Brady," he says, letting his voice fall into a touch of a drawl. He's a Southern boy but can hide the accent when he wants. Interesting. "I'm Brady Wilson."

He lifts my hand, but instead of kissing the back of it, he turns it over and presses his lips to my wrist.

My pulse jumps like crazy.

"I look forward to tonight," he says and lets me go.

Oh yes, *so do I.*

2: Brady the Bull Rider

The travel agent doesn't suspect a thing.

I get to my truck and climb into the cab. She was one sweet little number and flirty as all get out. I haven't saddled up with a girl like that in six states. Maybe I shouldn't have come on so strong, but she seemed into it.

Besides, I need her. I have to get on that cruise.

I don't have anything to hide really. But swinging a hundred thou on a cruise will set my bank account all the way back to my early bull-riding days, when the winnings were small and I had to sleep in my truck to get by.

Actually I've been sleeping in it anyway, driving to Miami straight from Houston, stopping only when

I flat out couldn't make another mile without running into a bar ditch.

I check the clock on the dash. I have all day until she gets off. I need to combine some accounts, pool my funds, and call that rodeo office in Nashville to find out where my last check is.

Fool's Errand. That was the bull in Nashville that put me over the top. And in the nick of time. I had no idea a chance to meet with a major sponsor was going to happen so fast. I'd been driving the wrong way, thinking I could find him in Houston. Thankfully, I'd overheard a conversation at a ranch where I was assessing a bull that the guy I wanted was going on this cruise.

His name is Adolfo Felini, and he manages one of the royal casinos in Monte Carlo. He's been looking for American sports stars to endorse beyond the Formula One racers that Monaco famously started.

I feel like bull riding is a perfect opportunity for that, and I've been ready to make a steady gig. I'm pushing thirty, and there's only so much tossing into the dirt a man's body should have to take. If I can get in with this Felini while I'm still a hot commodity on the circuit, we can parlay my dust crunching into training, endorsement deals, and I can be calling some shots myself at the major rodeos.

All the bureaucrats who looked down on the riders drawing the crowds will have to kiss *my* ass for a change.

Since the rodeos started getting televised, my purses have gone up. I began chasing this dream, and I'm willing to bet three years' savings that I can convince Felini that I'm his man.

It just takes getting on the cruise. I've tried a dozen other ways to get an appointment with him, but every door has been shut in my face.

Ten days on the water will give me time.

I make my calls, get some grub, and tool around Miami until it's time to head back to the travel agency.

Vivienne Carter. She was one beautiful woman. Her hair was the color of a sunset on a wheat field. Her eyes danced, and that mouth was made for kissing.

I'd paid particular attention to those breasts, though. She wanted me to look. I could see it heating her up. And I had no problem with politely obliging. I've peeled back that dress in my mind a hundred times since this morning.

If I get really lucky, that would be exactly the cherry on this ice cream sundae of a day.

I wonder about this screening she has to do.

Maybe she made it up. I went over the Blue Sapphire Yacht web site again on my phone earlier. It's two pages total. One nondescript landing screen with a picture of a boat and the name of the company. If you click on it, you go to a list of authorized agencies.

There are only ten. All in port towns, like they only want you booking if you can present yourself in person.

Vivienne said she needed to take my picture. Damn, they are tougher nuts than the TSA.

Maybe she'll let me return the favor. Imagining a sweet parting image of her delectable naked body on my phone gets me at half mast as I pull up to the glass front of the travel agency.

Cool your jets, Brady. Last thing I want to do is get my signals crossed and scare off the ticket onto this cruise to my future. I'll have to play it loose and easy and do only as much as the lady wants.

There's just one car in the lot now, a tiny white Chevy that has seen better days. The lights are mostly out inside, but I can see her. She has a desk lamp on, and it brightens her up like the moon on a clear night.

She's talking to someone, maybe on speaker. She doesn't have a phone to her ear. Or it's a Bluetooth too small for me to see. No one else seems to be inside.

When my dick is back in order, I head to the door. I don't think Vivienne has seen me. Since I can look in, the glass would be reflection for her. She's walking toward the back of the room. Sashaying, really, her hips swinging. Maybe there's music playing.

All the other desks are empty and dark. I tug on the door, half expecting it to be locked.

But it opens easily. As I pass through, Vivienne disappears into a room in the back. She leaves her door open, though, and at first I think I'm hearing a radio.

The voice is clear as a bell, soulful and sweet. I'm not familiar with the song, but it's about finding love and wishing it would last.

It starts to fade, and I glance around, looking for the source.

But then it pauses, there's a laugh, and it starts up again.

And I realize, it's the girl. She's singing.

The verse starts up again, growing louder as she walks back to the front room. She halts instantly when she sees me standing by the door.

"Oh!"

"Hey," I say.

She presses her palm to her mouth, her face pinking up. "I didn't know you were here!"

I hold out my hands. "Six, on the nose."

She points at the clock. "Five minutes till," she says. She pulls herself together and drops her hand. "I like a guy who's early."

"Then you're going to love me," I say. "And you're an amazing singer."

"Thanks," she says.

My eyes take her in. She's still in the green dress from earlier, only now I can see it all without the desk in between us. Just a simple tie holds it together. I picture tugging it loose and threaten to bulge out my jeans again.

She has this tiny waist and nice hips that fill out the dress. The skirt falls just to the knee, and curvy calves are pushed up by shoes that force me to tighten my jaw to stay in control. They're jet green and at least five inches high. Her coral-tipped toes peep out a little hole. I want to worship very inch.

The image of her naked in those shoes becomes my new life goal. I have to see it. Have to.

"You look beautiful," I say. Even though it's the same dress, I get the sense she added a little makeup and fixed her hair. I don't remember it being quite so perfect. "You have to close up tonight?"

She nods. Her lids droop a little, showing off her eyelashes. "I have the paperwork for you." She turns to her desk and bends over, picking up the pages.

Sweet Jesus. The skirt hikes considerably, revealing a long expanse of her thighs. I'm desperately interested in fitting in behind her and tearing whatever panties she's concealing right off her perfect ass.

Or maybe she doesn't have any. I have to force that thought aside or I'll be full mast in five seconds.

She turns around. "I have it all right here," she says, tucking the pages into a shiny folder with the agency logo on it. "We can fill it out at dinner."

"Do you have to do the picture here?" I ask, looking around for one of those pull-down screens, like at the DMV.

"Oh no. They aren't picky about it. I just have to certify that it's you."

I nod. She picks up a green purse and slides it to her shoulder. "You know your way around town?"

"I'm not from Miami," I say as I hold the door open for her.

She turns and locks it from the outside. "What do you like? Mexican? Cuban? Italian? Barbecue?"

Vivienne on a platter, I want to say, but remind myself of the goal. The cruise. "I'm easy. Probably not barbecue, though. I can't imagine Miami has anything on Texas for that."

"It would definitely be different," she says.

"There's a great pizza place nearby. Real wood-fired stuff. Great wine." She frowns. "And beer. You seem like a beer guy."

I laugh a little. "I can swing both ways," I say.

This makes her laugh, a ringing sound like a bell. "Good to know."

I open her door and she climbs in. My truck has a lift kit but nothing crazy. Still, she has to bend down to duck inside, and her ass is right in front of my face. God, she's killing me.

When she's settled, I close the door and head around. This is going to be one tough night keeping my hands off her until I get a definitive *go*. I'm hoping for it.

It's a short ride to the restaurant, and we get settled at a table right away. She gets her wine. I get beer. We laugh again.

Once the pizza is ordered, she spreads the pages out. It's been fairly businesslike so far, and this helps cool my jets.

"All right," she says. "Start working on this part with your standard name, address, and basics. You got a passport?"

"Yeah," I say, reaching behind to pull it from my back pocket. Thank goodness for that bull market in Mexico that forced me to apply for one. Fun one, too.

They raise incredible bulls there, and I was asked to assess some for a rodeo in Tucson.

She pulls a pen from her purse and passes it to me.

"So what do you do for a living?" she asks.

"This part of the screening?" I ask, giving her a grin.

"A little," she says. "Just making sure your cash crop isn't opium."

"I'm a professional bull rider."

"No shit!" she says, then claps her hand to her face. "My mama would wash my mouth out with soap."

"I like a girl who says what she means," I tell her.

"I have a potty mouth," she says. "I try to make it past the first date before I let the f-bombs fly."

"Do you usually succeed?" I ask.

She shrugs. "Not cussing or getting past the first date?"

She looks at me over her glass of wine, her eyebrows raised.

Is she saying men dump her after a single date? Or that *she* dumps *them*?

"I'm pretty flexible on either," I say, putting down my pen.

We look at each other for long moments, and I

have to admit, it's intense. Her eyes take in my face and my arms and shoulders. When she gets back to my eyes, I see that she's interested. I wish we didn't have a damn table between us.

She must feel the same, because she scoots over in the booth. "Come over to my side," she says.

My mama taught me to give a lady what she wants. I move around and sit beside her.

This is as close as we've been, and I get a good whiff of something subtle and sweet, like jasmine and vanilla. It's heaven. I pick up a piece of her pale hair, kissed with red. "This is the most glorious color I've ever seen."

She leans in, and I see we're not going to waste time. Her hand is on my thigh, and I meet her halfway. Her lips are soft and yielding, and I feel ready to devour her by the time I slide my tongue into her warm mouth.

And that's it. I already know she will be mine.

3: Vivienne

Holy hell, this boy is *hawt*.

I've been wanting my hands on him since he appeared in the door, and now I've got him.

Brady's mouth is warm and perfect. I could kiss him for five years straight.

My hand slides down his thigh in the jeans. He's muscled and hard. I imagine him on a bull and feel fire lick through me imagining how powerful those legs have to be.

A bull rider. Damn. That's definitely a new one for my list.

And yes, I do have a list.

His hand kneads the back of my neck, and I'm like a snowman in Louisiana, sliding into a puddle right there in Micky's Pizzeria. I want to lie down, feel him on top of me. And I want to see him. Every inch. Hopefully many inches.

The pizza arrives, but we take no note of it, diving into each other. His fingers tangle in my hair and I run a hand through his. So this is what his short curls feel like. I could die.

Well, not *yet*. We need to get to the main event. Then breathing will become optional.

His hand circles my leg. He grasps my knee and pulls it onto his lap, parting my thighs. Fingers make their way up, and I'm quivering. I want him there. I want him everywhere.

Someone clears their throat.

Ugh. Waitress.

"Shall I box this up to go?" she asks

I tear myself away from Brady. The girl has a pinched expression, probably from her hair being pulled back so tight.

"What do you think?" I ask him. "Should I eat you now or eat that later?"

His laugh tumbles out. "You are one naughty travel agent."

The girl flounces away.

"Okay, let's eat," I say. As much as I want this boy, I am starved. And a little anticipation is always good.

I slide my leg back to the floor. The air is charged, like we're building up to something amazing. I'm more turned on by this guy than anyone I've ever met.

"So tell me about the singing," he says. "Somebody with a voice like yours should be loved by millions."

"Try telling that to the labels I audition for," I say. I don't want a downer on the evening, so I add, "I have another trip to Memphis booked in the spring."

"Not Nashville?" he asks.

"Oh, I go there too," I say. I don't mention that most of those doors have been closed in my face already. "There's some smaller labels in Memphis."

"I take it by the destinations that you're going for the country music scene then?"

I nod. I generally don't go into it, as having to defend my choice can spoil a mood.

"I had a crush on Reba McEntire when I was a kid," he says. "She was a barrel racer and her dad roped steers." He laughs. "That was before my time, of course, but I have a lot of respect for girls who get out there and compete in the arena."

I gulp my wine. I am way too chicken-shit to do any of that. My heart drops. He's probably been in

25

love with a million girls way tougher and more interesting than me.

I fiddle with my wine glass, turning it in circles. A shame wave comes over me. I hate those. They are unexpected and torrential.

They make me feel like I'm hopeless. Nobody wants me to sing for them. I'm not a skinny girl like Faith or Shania. I don't do anything interesting except book people on trips they can't really afford.

He reaches under the table to grab my hand. "Hey, Vivienne. What's wrong?"

I shrug. The shame wave is pretty debilitating when it comes. I especially hate it when it washes over me with a new man. Usually I can ride my high for a few hours.

Case in point number five: I fake ninety percent of my confidence.

And it's run off like a floozy with a Bible salesman.

I can't help it. It's just this guy is so awesome. Charming. Sexy. Strong. And here I'm blowing it with my damn insecurities.

His fingers encircle mine. "There's lots of ways to be amazing," he says. "I take my hat off to anyone with the guts to follow their passion."

I still can only shrug. But the shame wave retreats

a bit, heading back up the shore.

"People think I have guts getting on a bull," he says. "And yeah, maybe I'm risking my bones. But I think about you. Going in front of all those strangers to sing, knowing that they're probably going to turn you down. That's just about the gutsiest thing I've ever heard. I can't believe I'm sitting next to a girl with a dream like that."

The shame wave is in full retreat now, headed back into low tide. I sit up a little straighter.

"You had a lot of people say no?" he asks. His eyes are gentle, and I'm a puddle all over again.

"Sixty-four," I say.

I have a list for that too.

Case in point number six: I always aim to keep the number of men I've slept with higher than the number of record execs who have turned me down.

It's how I get by.

Don't judge me now. You're already on chapter three. It's too late to quit.

"Damn," Brady says. "I've only been thrown by fifty-seven bulls in public. So you've got me beat."

I can feel the smile coming on. The sun is out again, and I'm on that beach in a polka dot bikini, the shame wave lost in the sparkle of the sea.

"Nobody's going to make me give up on my

dream," I say.

He slides a slice of pizza off the tray to my plate. "Tell me what got you singing."

"My gramma," I say, watching with a bit of envy as the tip of pizza disappears between his glorious lips. "She always said I could sing with the angels. Got me in the church choir and singing solos."

"Church choir," Brady says. "Now that's a picture."

I guess he means compared to the way we were PDAing our way onto the waitress's bad side a few minutes ago. It's fine. I made peace with my lack of Bible behavior years ago.

"You should see me in a shorty choir robe," I say. "Naked underneath."

He chokes a little, and I smack his back. I forget I've just met this boy today. I'm way too comfortable around him.

When he stops coughing, I fold my pizza and take a big bite. His eyes stay on my lips, like I thought they might. I mean, if his open mouth got to me, it made sense I would get to him.

My heart is racing, and this is the feeling I love the most. New boy. Anticipation. All the promise and discovery with none of the disappointment that might come later.

It's all brand new.

The chitchat is pretty easy after that. Brady talks about rodeo life, what makes a feisty bull, and how he gets the grit together to ride on the back of a thousand pounds of snorting, angry meat.

He's gotten busted up a few times, but nothing big. Broken arm twice, snapped his collar bone once.

"I'm lucky that I have an eye for a good bull," he says. "So I often get called in to help pick stud bulls for breeding."

"Sounds like a crazy life," I say.

"What's the craziest thing that's ever happened in an audition?" he asks. "Do men try to take advantage of you?"

I see a flash in his eye that I like. As if he's worried. Like he might pummel somebody who tried to put one over on me.

"It's not as common as everyone thinks," I say. "The big labels, they are all pros. Mostly they're cold as ice."

"How do you get an audition?"

It's cute how interested he is. I admit that more than my girl parts are engaged now. He might be opening my heart up a little.

"Same way anybody does. I check for open calls. Get notifications if one of the talent TV shows will be filming tryouts. Put stuff on YouTube and hope it catches fire."

"You're on YouTube?" He's got his phone out before I can shut my trap.

"Oh, don't," I say. "I use a fake name."

He sets the phone on the table. "I'll respect that," he says. "But I have some fans of my own. They're the right demographic. They might help pass it around."

I shrug. I've had people say they'll help me before. I've paid for ads. I've tried everything. It's one of the reasons I'm so poor. Between flights to Nashville and recording booths and sponsored videos, it's an expensive dream.

I just can't get anywhere.

He tucks his phone away again. "I liked what I heard earlier," he says, taking another bite of pizza.

We eat in silence for a bit and I sip the wine. The evening's about to move on. We were all hot and heavy earlier, but something's shifted. We're all serious.

I can cure that.

"Come with me somewhere," I say. "I'll sing for you."

His eyebrows rise. "Let's go!"

He tosses some money on the table, and I gather

all the papers into the folder again. We're done on that, other than the picture.

"Wait a sec," I say.

He pauses, turning back to me.

The light is just right, bright on one side. He looks brooding, sexy, and perfect.

"Let me get a quick pic of you before I forget."

He stands straighter.

I unlock my phone and take a quick shot. It's devastating, that smile, those dark blue eyes, that sandy hair that curls just enough to give it a wave.

Blue Sapphire Yachts will snap him up.

We load up in his truck, and I direct him down back roads and through shady neighborhoods until we arrive at FreakEasy, a hole-in-the-wall bar with a dirt parking lot. It's surrounded with cars, even on a weeknight.

A big banner reads, "Live streamed karaoke every Monday." And that's what we're here for. The best amateur singers in Miami come here, and it's not unheard of for real singing stars to drop in and join you in a number if you happen to choose one of their songs. I saw Dylan Wolf jump in on "Blue Shoes" once, and everybody in the crowd just about died.

"Now this looks like real Miami," Brady says.

"It is," I tell him.

As we walk in, I run through my mental playlist, trying to figure out what song would be a sure thing to reel in this masterpiece.

Not that I think it's in question.

But I don't like to take any chances.

Brady opens the door and a song washes over us. It's a guy I know, probably somewhere around number forty-two (don't judge me)! We tried dating regular, but turns out the magic only happened once. Since then, if we bump into each other at the bar, we just raise a glass to each other after a song.

No hard feelings.

He's singing "Sign on the Door," which generally means he's dumped a girl again. Probably the morose ex is here somewhere. We could all take a picture together. That would be a lark.

I really should expand my scene, but this bar is comfortable and it's like "Cheers," everybody here knows my name.

And a few of them, a *bit* more than that.

Still, it feels good as we head to the bar and I'm greeted by at least a dozen people on the way. The guys nod, eyes on Brady, and the girls tilt their heads, nodding in approval.

A couple ask me what I'm singing tonight.

I haven't decided yet.

Carl is behind the bar. He's tall and muscled and doesn't have a number on my list, by the way. He's into men.

"Wine or whisky tonight?" he asks.

I glance over at Brady. "You do shots?"

"I do tonight," he says.

Carl nods and serves up a couple glasses of Jameson's.

Brady picks them both up and passes one to me. We clink the short glasses together and toss them back. It's fire down my throat, and by the time I've recovered, I know what I'm singing.

"Be right back," I tell Brady as he orders another round. I wind my way over to Mariah, who runs the karaoke machine.

Three girls are giggling at the mic, waiting for their song to start. It will be "Wild Thing" or "Baby Got Back" no doubt. Drunk girl anthems. If one of them is on the rebound, she'll have them all sing "Before He Cheats."

But when the song begins, it's worse, actually. "Mmmbop."

There's a collective groan.

I turn to Mariah. She's grooving to the song, big black headphones smashing her wild electric blue hair. She likes everything.

"Whatcha got tonight?" she asks me.

"Keep Me Up All Night." I have to shout a little to be heard.

Mariah's eyebrows lift. "You haven't done that one before."

"I brought a new boy."

She nods knowingly. "I'll bump you in after these girls," she says. "We need something decent after this." She tilts her head at the stage, where the girls are squealing their "Mmmbops" and dissolving into giggles.

Mariah gets super annoyed when tourists figure out how to get to her karaoke and muck it up. She won't rotate them back in for hours, if at all, if they aren't singing proper.

I head back to Brady. He hands me a second shot.

God, he looks good here. The colored lights dance across the hard lines of his face. I don't often bring dates to this place. It's my sacred stomping ground, and after getting unlucky with a one-night stand that became a stalker, I'm super careful about bringing strangers here. I can't get pushed out of the one place I truly call home.

Case in point number seven: I sometimes inspire cult-like devotion.

It's the singing. It's like a super power. I'm not saying I'm great or anything. But there's emotion in song, and when you combine the right song with the right voice at just the right moment in time, there's magic there.

I'm hoping to hit that combo tonight.

"Mmmbop" finally ends and I squeeze Brady's hand. "I'm up," I say.

I lead him closer to the stage and leave him leaning against the end of the bar.

Mariah hands me a microphone. "Knock 'em dead."

I intend to. At least one of them.

I take the sleek black mic and step into the spotlight. Mariah changes the lights to pure white, so the bar is dotted with stars as the opening chords begin.

Since I'm telling you this story, listen up. If your phone is close by, go on and head to YouTube and find the song I'm about to sing. It's called "Keep Me Up All Night" if you missed it when I told Mariah.

The version you hear won't be me singing. I haven't made a video with it. But Julie Roberts has an incredible version, and her voice isn't so different from mine.

I'll wait, mic in hand.

Got it?

Okay.

The opening licks start up.

The first few lines are soulful, and I sing them dark and low, looking out over the crowd. Only when the first verse is about over do I turn and find Brady.

The lights cascade over him. He's smiling at me, and when our eyes lock, I forget anyone else is in the room. I sing right to him.

The new feeling washes over me. It's the exact opposite of the shame wave. It's blues and fire and soul. It's me, it's him, it's the bodies swaying. It's the music and the words and the connection between voice and spirit.

That magic happens, and I realize my eyes are closed. I open them again and slide my gaze across the shimmering people who are watching me sing, and I rest again on Brady.

He's stock still, watching me. And it's there. I want him. We're one person riding this wave together.

This is what I live for. The music, the sound, the people. And having one person you're doing it all for. It doesn't matter that Brady is a client and this is just for one night. It still feels good.

I sing that killer line for him one more time, "Keep me up all night."

The last notes fade out and the crowd erupts. I give a little bow and hand the mic to Mariah.

"I'll rotate you back in whenever you like," she says. "But it looks like you'll be busy."

Oh, I *will*.

4: Brady the Bull Rider

I'm completely overwhelmed by this woman.

Beautiful. Funny. Bright.

And that voice.

I have to have her.

Have to.

Vivienne pushes through the crowd to get to me. Everybody wants a piece of her, reaching out, calling out, trying to get her attention.

But her eyes are on me.

Damn.

When she gets to me, I can't even find words for how I feel about her song.

So I put my hand on her back and pull her in super close. Her body is warm and soft against me. My fingers brush her waist.

Vivienne looks up at me. Her eyes shine. Her hair glows a gentle gold-red from the light. I lean down, my lips landing on hers in a gentle kiss. We're in her world now, among people she knows. I don't want to upset the balance of her life here.

But her arms come up around my neck. A few people let out a whoop as we press closer together, my mouth insistent now, diving into her.

She picked that song. I know she must mean it. The connection between us is vibrant, like a lasso around us. She tastes of whisky, and I want to drown in it, more intoxicated by her than the drink.

Her breasts press up against me, and I have to fight for control. We're surrounded, and the music fires up again, another girl hoping to sing like Vivienne but falling sorely short.

She breaks the kiss, gasping a little. "We can go," she says. "I'm ready to go."

I'm not sure where we're headed yet, but I hang on and lead her back outside.

By the truck, I can't wait to kiss her again. There's no one watching now, and I touch her more freely, hungry as a bull, my hand sliding up her thigh.

She lifts her leg up and around me. I close in, raging with need, and press my rock-hard cock against her.

She moans against my mouth. "I have two roommates," she says. "One is a homebody. You have a hotel?"

"I do." It's not fancy, especially not for someone buying a six-figure cruise. I wonder if she expects something grand, assuming I'm rich.

"It's not much," I say, but she kisses me again.

I open her door, kissing her as I lift her up on the seat. I reluctantly break away to step back. God, I hope she's not a gold digger who dumps me when she realizes I'm not Mr. Money Bags.

I feel more anxious than I let on as we drive back to the main road. She turns on the radio and hums along with a Taylor Swift song.

Pulling up to the motel will either kill what's happening or it won't. I brace myself for her reaction as I turn on my blinker. She nods along to the music.

I park and wait for her to notice where we are. But she just opens her door and steps out, then peers back in.

"You shy or something?" she asks with grin.

And that's it. I jump out lightning fast and race around to her. I take her hand, and we fairly run up the metal steps to the second floor. I fumble with the key card as she looks around.

"I used to have an apartment about a block from

here," she says. "When I first arrived."

I wrestle the door open, flooded with relief that she doesn't care. That it's about us after all.

She steps in.

The only light is low to the ground, plugged into a socket near the floor. It illuminates those killer shoes, and I'm dying for that image in my head to be real.

I shut the door and turn to her. We're two shadows at first, but gradually my eyes adjust. She sets her purse on the dresser and leans against the edge of it.

"What first?" she asks.

"I want to see the body that fits that angel voice," I say. "Strip for me."

She tilts her head. "Piece for piece."

"Fair enough."

"You start," she says.

I unbutton the flannel shirt, watching her. She has her hands propped on the dresser behind her, making her breasts stand at beautiful attention. I'm desperate to see them, touch them, feast on them.

But I take my time. Her voice is still in my head, the image of her on that stage, singing for me. How stupid are those recording execs? They have no idea what they are missing.

I toss the shirt on a chair.

She can't be wearing much. She reaches for a shoe, but I stop her. "Can those be last?" I ask.

"Sure," she says. She hesitates, and I realize her dress is all one piece. But she gives me a sly smile and reaches beneath her skirt. With a small tug, a piece of green silk slides down.

Her panties.

My cock strains against my jeans. Jesus.

She tosses them to me, and I press them to my face. They smell divine, like detergent and floral lotion and her. God, I want to bury myself between those legs.

I'm dying.

I kick my boots off. "Don't count," I say, "since I asked yours to stay on."

She shrugs.

I grab the collar of my undershirt and pull it off my head. When it clears and I've tossed it on the chair, I see Vivienne looking at me.

She likes what she sees.

I'm practically salivating, waiting to see what will come next.

She tosses me a flirty grin and reaches behind her. Then pushes beneath her dress at the shoulder.

A strap peeps out from the bottom of a sleeve,

and she tugs it down her elbow and off her arm.

What is she doing?

She repeats the process on the other arm, then reaches into her cleavage.

A shiny green bra emerges.

"Now that's talent," I say, catching the garment as she tosses it to me.

"I have many."

Her nipples are visible beneath the fabric of her dress now. She's naked beneath it.

I unzip my jeans, glad to be rid of the damn things. My boxers tent out instantly, and when I glance at Vivienne, all her attention is on my crotch.

The jeans drop, and I make sure my socks go with them as I kick them off.

"Your turn," I say. My cock strains with need as she looks at me. Her naked in the shoes. I'm about to get there.

"You untie it," she says. "Like a present."

I walk straight up to her. I want to hold on to this incredible moment, as intense as when she sang to me.

I touch her wrists, bent against the dresser still. My fingers glide up her bare arms to the sleeves of the dress. Then across her shoulders, lightly fluttering across her collarbone.

They flirt with the edge of the dress as it makes a V down to her breasts.

Her breathing gets shallow as I take my time. I cup the sides of the curves, then with aching slowness, allow my thumbs to cross those pert nipples beneath the fabric.

She sucks in a breath, her head falling back. I can't resist her neck, open to me, and press my mouth to it.

She arches up to me, and I slip the dress off her shoulder. It slides down easily, revealing the first tempting breast.

My fire is raging, but I force myself to take my time. I kiss slowly down her neck until I reach the swell. Her breast is heavy and luscious and full. I lift it to me as my mouth captures the nipple.

I suckle greedily, still not looking yet, but learning her by feel and taste. She smells divine. My finger reaches for the tie, and with a sharp tug, it comes free.

I pull away as it falls, my eyes taking her in.

The fabric glides down her body like a caress.

She's a goddess, all curves and valleys, glowing skin and warmth.

I don't know what I want next, where to taste her, what to touch.

I take both her hands and hold them out,

stepping back to take all of her in. Her breasts are high and round, her waist dainty, hips full. Her thighs fall together, and I want them apart, to dive there.

But I only look, down, down to those lovely legs ending in those killer shoes.

"I want to worship you," I say, and move close, frenzied, hands on her breasts. I kiss my way around her body, touching her waist, her back, her shoulders, completely lost in her skin.

I come around to the front again and lean in, my lips almost grazing hers. "Spread those legs for me," I say.

She obeys and the gates open, pale silken hair in only a tiny thatch above those swollen pink folds.

My finger slides along them, and she grasps my head, almost losing her balance. I push her back to the dresser and lift her by the thighs so that she sits on it. Now those shoes are off the ground ,and I spread her knees wide.

She leans back, those beautiful breasts pointed high.

I can't wait but just dive between those thighs with fingers, mouth, and tongue. She's hot and seeking, pulsing around me. Her sweet nub vibrates as I work it, and her legs quiver with need.

My mouth moves with her, fingers setting the

pace. I listen to the sounds she makes, as glorious as her song, and move her up the scale.

We work together in perfect sync, her body, my work. Her hands grasp my shoulders, and every muscle in her tenses.

I push just a touch harder, and she's over the top, crying, laughing, calling my name. I extend her out until she's gasping for breath, then bring her down gently, her thighs settling back on the dresser.

"Oh my God," she says. "Jesus, hellfire, and brimstone."

Yeah, this girl goes to church.

I kiss my way down her thigh and ease her up. She hangs on to me, her head on my shoulder.

Carefully, I bend down to slide her shoes off, then pick her up and carry her over to the bed.

She curls into me as I settle next to her. "Give me a minute," she says. "I've had my mind blown."

I wait for her as she slows her breath, her fingers tracing their way along my chest and belly.

My cock jumps in the blue boxers, and she moves her hand down.

"I'm really looking forward to this," she says.

"It's all yours," I tell her.

She shifts to her knees and slides her fingers in the waistband. The cool air hits my skin as she peels them down.

Her exhale as my cock lifts up to her pleases me. She likes what she sees.

She tosses the boxers and turns to straddle my knees.

The view is incredible, her breasts swaying lazily over my dick, her hair floating like a cloud. I can't take a picture so I embed the image on my brain.

"I am going to feast on this," she says, taking my cock in her hand.

"Be my guest," I say.

And she does.

5: Vivienne

Oh, man. I'm in love with a dick.
It's glorious.
I could write a song about it.
Maybe I will.

I only met you just today
All eight (nine?) inches of you
But by the time I'm through
I may only like the man you serve
But I'll be in love with you.

Ha. I kill myself.
But really, it's one seriously song-inspiring boner.
I take my time with it, fingers wrapped around its

girth. I slide along the length. I don't know if cowboy here manscapes, but there's a nice bit of hair at the base, and none anywhere else. The chest is smooth, the belly and below.

It's damn perfect.

Brady watches for a moment, then gives in and rocks his head back. I let one hand slide along his chest. God, he's a specimen. I like boys in general and I'm not super picky. But this one is exceptional. There's not an ounce of fat on him.

The end of my new favorite toy gets a little shiny, and even though it's probably not in my best safety interest, I lean in to taste it. Once I start, there is no stopping. I pull as much of that beefy cock into my mouth and slip it a little down my throat.

He groans and that's all the encouragement I need.

I intend to work him over a while, then see about a condom for a little more action. But I'm having too much fun. He grabs my waist and flips me around, burying his face between my legs a second time.

Good God. I keep going so he'll keep going. It's too damn amazing. He's got the gift, and I'm already tensing up down there for another go.

I want to give as good as I'm getting, so I work him hard, as deep as I can. He throbs against my mouth.

I never want any of this to end, but my body is ready for round two to come to the mountaintop. I'm spiraling up, everything tensing in anticipation.

And then it all lets go, my body releasing. I feel high, like a kite on the Fourth of July, fireworks going off all around. I push him a little harder, and he's over the edge too, spilling everywhere, bubbling over like a fountain.

I slip to the side so we can both breathe, but don't turn around yet. My arms are shaky, and I feel wrung out, like my body has outdone itself.

After a moment, Brady sits up and pulls me around to fit me against his shoulder. My hair is everywhere, but he tenderly smooths it away from my face and tucks it back.

I'm a little hot with shock over how I'm feeling. I mean this is number seventy-two, and I only met him today. I am super good at separating the sex from the heart.

It was good sex.

That has to be enough.

I talk myself down and don't look up at him until I know I don't have love-struck googly eyes anymore.

He smiles down at me. "You are a gift."

Well, hell. I have to look down again as another

wave of emotion crashes over me. What is wrong with me? I must be ovulating or something. Those hormones mess with your head.

But it feels good right here.

We get quiet, the sounds of the motel filtering into the room. A TV a few doors down. A motorcycle driving by. Someone laughs in the parking lot.

It's cozy.

"Sing me something," Brady says.

I shift against him. He's not the first to ask that. I have a fairly deep post-coital repertoire. All sort of up tempo. Nothing too soft and romantic. I don't want to appear all lovestruck, and I have a stalker problem already.

My go-to is "Nothing On But the Radio."

But I just can't make it start. It's all wrong. Too fast. Too laid-back.

So I do something I shouldn't.

I pull out a little Faith Hill.

And I sing "Breathe."

Go ahead, pull it up. You probably know it.

It's way too revealing. Too breathless.

But I just can't help it.

This guy is inspiring me.

I have to sit up a little to sing. His hand slides up and down my arm as I do it.

He looks amazing, lying there against the white sheets, his head denting the pillow. Like an Adonis. Like a husband. Like home.

My throat tries to close up, but I push through. His eyes don't leave my face. I brace myself with a hand on his chest, warm and muscled and perfect.

I have to stop after the second verse. I just can't do this. It's messing with my head. I fade the song out and lie down.

"You are the most amazing thing I've ever heard," he says. He shifts me more comfortably against him.

I don't talk any more. I'm trying to sort out all the things I'm feeling. After a while of my silence, his breathing gets all even.

I know it's chicken-shit, but as soon as he's solidly out, I slip away from him. I wrap the dress around me without even bothering with the underwear. I stuff my panties and bra in my purse and pick up the folder with his application for the cruise.

Brady rolls over when the door clicks, but he doesn't seem to wake. Or maybe he's a gentleman all the way and just lets me go.

My car's still at the agency, but it's only a couple miles away. I'll call a Lyft ride since it will only be a few dollars. I'd walk it if it weren't for the dang shoes.

I might see him again if he pays in person, but it's not necessary. He can send it online now that the paperwork is done.

He's a perfect human.

I'm an imperfect girl.

So I tiptoe away and head back to life as it was meant to be for me.

6: Brady the Bull Rider

I'm used to being an early riser on the ranch, so I'm up before dawn.

I know Vivienne is gone. I felt her leave the bed and watched her sneak out with hooded eyes.

I was torn between getting up to take her home and letting her go on her own terms.

She seemed so distressed that I felt it best to let her be. She called out to somebody right outside the door, so I knew she grabbed a ride. I didn't jump out there and make her let me take her home.

Maybe I should have.

But hard as it was, I let her go.

The sheets get cold as soon as I leave them. Might as well start this day. Vivienne has all my info, so she can let me know if I get on the cruise.

In the meantime, I have to get hold of Nashville and track down the missing check. I need all my assets to make it on that cruise.

If I don't get on, I'm not sure what's next. Another rodeo, another purse, another shot at getting thrown and ending up injured and out of the game before I'm ready.

The circuit fires up again in a few months. Before that can happen, I have to find this Adolfo Felini guy, convince him that I'm a good bet, and be on my way to the next phase.

But it's Vivienne who keeps stealing my attention as I shower and go about my day. That sunset hair. That curvy figure. The image of her in the green shoes will not be leaving my head any time soon.

Passionate. Really bold. Everything perfect.

And that voice.

I don't know what spooked her, what made her sneak out in the middle of the night. I get the idea that she's used to short romances. But if that's her choice or she cuts off rejection before it can come, I'm not sure.

Maybe when I filled out that paperwork, she saw I lived far off. I couldn't be that much to her. We both knew that, underneath it all. Miami is just a means to an end.

I wish I could have at least gotten the name she used on YouTube. I would have made good on my promise to send out her video to my fans. There's several thousand people who follow me, and they'd love her.

Maybe when she emails me about the cruise, I'll ask.

And if I'm really lucky, I can convince her to see me one more time.

I'm not one to stalk a lady who is done with me. I'll keep it strictly business until I can figure out if I have a chance with her again.

And I sure hope I do.

7: Vivienne

God, that walk of shame was worse than usual.

I got my ride, braless and panty-less, to my crappy car. It gets pretty cold at night, and my old Chevy wouldn't start up.

The driver was nice, hanging out to make sure I could get it going. The cold meant my nipples were literally two south poles in the dress. He kept spotting them and blushing.

And of course, my panties *would* fall out of my purse.

God.

Even my forward-thinking gramma would have shaken her head at this one.

Thankfully, the car eventually starts, and I get home and sleep a couple hours before having to get up and make it in to the agency.

Sam is already there, and bless her, she's got two hot lattes ready, both for me.

"Girl, you look like something the cat drug in," she says. "Tell me he was wicked hot."

I gulp coffee first, the scald in my throat as welcome as a hot shower on a cold morning.

Sam waits, twisting a curl around her pencil. She got a new weave after work yesterday, and it's killer. The curls against her dark skin are divine. She looks like a model. Watching her make this transition has been awe-inspiring to me.

I love her to death.

"You have your caffeine, now spill," she says.

"Your hair is fantastic," I tell her.

"I know," she says. "Best extensions money can buy. Now give it up about cowboy."

"We got pizza. I sang for him."

"What song?"

"Keep Me Up All Night."

"Girl!" she squeals loudly enough that Janet in the back turns to look.

Sam gets up and moves closer, sitting her cute butt in a gold pencil skirt on my desk. She definitely does hot working girl better than I do. I'm a lost cause today in a paisley grandma dress and my hair in a messy bun. It's all I could manage.

"Then we went to his hotel," I say.

Sam leans in. "And…"

"We did…stuff." It occurs to me that we didn't actually do the deed. And that maybe we planned to. But we were so caught up in that simultaneous sixty-nine climax that we didn't keep going.

It was my fault, I think. I got all love gushy, then pulled away. I'm sure Brady thought I was half crazy.

The shame wave threatens to overtake my shores, and I gulp the rest of latte number one.

Sam is my hero.

The rush of caffeine hits, and I'm able to focus a little better.

"Well," Sam says, getting impatient. "Was it good stuff?"

"Yeah," I say, closing my eyes and holding the warm cup to my forehead. "It was real good."

"What's that, sixty-something?" she asks.

For a minute I think she's figured out the sixty-nine, but then I remember she knows about The List.

"Seventy-two," I say.

"Damn, girl. You are my idol." She slides off the desk and lifts her arms in the air. "I bow to your abundance. Your copulation cornucopia. Your plentiful pricks." She bends with a flourish of hand waves.

I shake my head. My mama would shit herself.

Gramma might laugh.

Still, I'm feeling a bit lost.

I liked him.

But I have ambitions.

And where does it all lead? Let's say I call him up, see him again. He's just here to get on a boat. Then he'll be gone.

Better to end on my terms.

Better one great night than a few more mediocre ones that create diminishing returns.

Although getting him between the legs might have been nice.

Stupid love gushy me.

Although *he* was the one who pulled me in and asked me to sing.

I shake my head to rid my thoughts of him and turn on my computer.

I've got a notice from Blue Sapphire Yachts. I figure it's from the request I placed for the Cayman cruise, but when I click it, it's a referral.

I scan the email. Some secretary submitting on behalf of her boss. He's a first-timer on Sapphire.

I write her saying I need to do a screening in person since he hasn't cruised before.

She replies immediately in all caps that MITCH ROBERTS DOES NOT DO SCREENINGS.

This is going to take finishing my second latte before I can reply politely.

"Hey," I say to Sam. "You been getting any Blue Sapphire Yacht referrals?" I wonder if I should pass this one to her.

She shrugs. "Nope. They don't come along often, and when they do, they tend to play favorites."

Sam has been at this longer than me, four years to my two. It's true I did a couple Sapphire bookings earlier this year. I guess they liked my work, not that filling out a screening is any big deal.

I turn back to the email. Sigh. Bigwigs. I guess maybe it does take the right touch to handle some of them without tweaking their nose. And it IS a big commission. If I get two in one month, that will more than pay for my next audition trip.

My reply makes my nose browner than a mountain in a mudslide. I explain that only the most elite of travelers is even considered a candidate for Blue Sapphire Yachts. What an extraordinary trip it will be!

I roll my eyes, tacking on some yada yada about how her boss is also protected by this policy, as none of the riffraff gets in by pretending to be Prince

Harry.

There's a pause after this one. She's either thinking it over or doing something else.

I turn back to Brady's application and pull up the screen to type the info. His handwriting is small and neat. Once that's all in, I tug out my phone and find his picture.

This makes me pause. So handsome. I see that face disappearing between my thighs again. A long sigh escapes. Seventy-two was definitely one for the record books. I email the image to my work address and pick it up on the screen to attach to the application.

Once he's approved, I'll get his deposit via the secure site and then the final payment. Technically, I don't have to see him again.

The rest of the day is like most of the days before. A lot of sittin' around. I don't hear from the snooty secretary. Maybe her boss has a black past and couldn't pass muster.

Literally. Muster. Like on a ship.

I kill myself.

I go home, think about Brady. No telling where he is.

I Netflix myself to sleep and prepare for another day of drudgery. At least I can look forward to karaoke night. I'm a star there. That's more than a lot of people have got.

When I log in at the agency the next morning, a couple emails come through. A confirmation of the application for Brady.

And the snooty secretary has replied finally, *telling* me, not asking, that Mitch Roberts will send a car to take me to his office at precisely 1:00 p.m. tomorrow.

Huh. Like I have that much time in my day to go gallivanting off who knows where to do a screening. Like I care if he gets on the boat.

Although I do. It's worth serious cash.

But still. Rich people can kiss my shiny white butt.

I'm about to fire back something of that nature when I see the address at the bottom of her email footer.

Maybe I should just check where he is.

My jaw drops when I see the building. It's the tippy top of the tallest office building on the bay. It's not far from the cruise ports, actually. I could make a lovely day of it.

Hmmm. There's a restaurant in his building that is impossible to get reservations for.

I laugh a little to myself as I write back.

I can only take time away from the office for that length if we can squeeze in a lunch. La Traviata is in the same building. How about we meet there?

I tap my fingers on the desktop as I wait for a reply. Sam has come in and sits filing her nails. Janet has her feet up and is doing Sudoku.

Yeah, we're real busy.

But *Mitch Roberts* doesn't know that. Or his secretary. I picture a weasel-faced old man in a suit with flared nostrils and a bad attitude about peasants like me.

Of course, he *could* be a Christian Grey.

I sit up a little straighter. He might be worth a Google.

The search results are fascinating. Mitch Roberts is self-made and has a net worth of $3.2 billion.

I think I might have 3.2 *dollars* in my checking account.

He's good friends with another self-made billionaire, Dell Brant, and the two of them are known as the "Kings of Start-Ups" for always knowing which new companies are prime for investment. There's a picture of the two of them shaking hands, and honestly, either one would do.

But when I switch over to images, it's clear which

one is Mitch. He's tall, lean, sort of Adam Levine-esque. His hair is short and dark. There are no pictures of him laughing. Or smiling. Or with a woman.

Gay?

I switch back to the bio. Never married. Seen with a few key models here and there, not big on the spotlight. A bit reclusive.

Huh.

I stare at the image again. He scares me, a little. And I just insisted on lunch with him.

I'm about to back out of that part when my email chimes. It's secretary.

Yes, she says. La Traviata is fine. 1:00 reservation. Since this would be a second lunch for Mr. Roberts, in the interest of saving time, would I please review the menu so she could order for us in advance? That way they could get me back to work more swiftly.

I laugh out loud. Well, okay, why not?

I pull up the link to the menu. I plan to order the most expensive things, but there are no prices. I choose some oysters, a lasagna, a decadent torte, and both an aperitif and digestif, which I recently learned are fancy drinks to be taken before and after a meal. I pick whatever sounds interesting.

I hit send with flourish.

"What's got you all flouncy?" Sam asks.

"I'm going to La Traviata for lunch tomorrow," I say.

"Get out!" Her curls fly as she whips her head around. "How did you score that?"

"Some billionaire wanting a Blue Sapphire Yacht."

"Damn!" Sam smacks her hand on the desk. "You're sending me the next one."

"Totally," I say. "It's been months since I've booked one, and now I have two."

"Sweet deal," she says. "Who's the guy?"

I roll my chair over to her desk, and we spend the afternoon drooling over what images we can find of Mitch Roberts.

Maybe I've found number seventy-three.

8: Mitch the Billionaire

I'm vexed as hell when I realize Bonnie has booked me a double lunch on the day.

"Think of it as a break," she says as she runs a roller across my suit sleeves. This is standard procedure of late, because my cat Belle has been ill and I've been bringing her to work. I don't really trust anyone to watch her properly after the cat-sitter I hired didn't even notice she'd thrown up both her meals under the divan.

She's sleeping on her little red throne Bonnie ordered to match the decor of my office. I couldn't give a damn about that, but the cat does look rather regal with her long white Persian fur spread along the velvet.

Fur Bonnie is extracting from my suit now.

Damn stuff gets everywhere.

"You'll stay with her?" I ask Bonnie.

"Of course," she says. "She'll be fit as a fiddle under my watch."

"All right. Thank you."

"It's adorable how much you care for her," Bonnie says and opens the door for me.

I can see the amusement in her eyes. I'm aware several members of the staff are laughing at me, the serious bachelor businessman feeling sentimental over an old cat.

My shoes rap smartly against the tile floor as I head to the elevator.

What they don't know, and what I won't tell them, is that Belle belonged to my mother, who died ten years ago. My sister Amelia took her, but then decided to join the Peace Corps. And so Belle came to me.

Belle is on in years, a full eighteen now, and I will not see her fall ill while Amelia is gone. My sister considers Belle the last thing of our mother's that matters. I won't have the cat dying on my shift.

Besides, I was there when Mother breathed her last, Belle cuddled up to her side. Looking at the cat made it easier for all of us to manage those final moments.

She's a good kitty.

I tug on my cuffs as the elevator descends to the bottom floor. I had a light lunch with five fellows from Switzerland earlier today, so I will keep this one short and to the point.

But it is crucial. I booked an exclusive cruise to meet an incredibly important contact. I may not actually go, as the deal is pending a meeting later today. But I want to ensure I can get on it should everything work out.

This woman, whoever she is, demanding we have lunch, is the only thing standing in the way of my ticket. I'll charm her swiftly, jump through whatever silly hoops her agency requires to get me approved, and be on with my day.

I pat my jacket pocket, ensuring I have my passport. It's there. Bonnie, for all her faults, is most proficient in ensuring all goes smoothly.

This meeting will be no different.

The elevator opens into a bustling atrium, awash with light from a thousand window panes facing the bay. I've enjoyed having an office that looks out onto the ocean, even if the view is somewhat cluttered by the tiny keys and cruise ports.

So different than my Georgia upbringing. Miami has been a pleasant balance between my Southern roots and the need for a port city for my trade. Unlike my friend Dell, who loves New York and its tight spaces, I prefer open sky.

As I cross, I spot a colorful young woman wandering the atrium, looking around as though she's never seen anything like it.

"I just got here in a limo," she tells a random passerby. "See that black one outside there? That's the one."

The man nods politely and moves on. She's undeterred by his lack of interest. She clasps her hands and stares out at the ocean. "This is why I came here," she says to no one in particular.

Something about her makes me pause to watch. She's lovely and fresh, maybe twenty-five. Her hair is blond with reddish highlights, like strawberries and cream.

Her dress is deep blue at the top, gradually shifting in hue to emerald green at the bottom. She's like a jewel herself, her happiness sparkling like the water she can't take her gaze from.

The crystal clock tower in the center of the room strikes one. She jumps a little, her eyes wide. "Shoot, where in tarnation is it?"

I hear the Southern note in her voice and walk over to her.

"Can I be of service?"

She sees me, and her eyes get even bigger. "You look an awful lot like Mitch Roberts."

I'm taken aback. I'm not the sort of person who is recognized by random people, only my employees and business partners.

"That might be because I *am* Mitch Roberts."

She laughs with a nice ring that almost makes me crack a smile.

"Then I'm not late!" She slides her arm right through mine. "I'm your date for lunch!"

Her familiarity is more than a little surprising. Most people keep their distance from me. I'm not known for my friendliness.

But she doesn't seem to know or care.

"I'm Vivienne Carter," she says. "Your ticket to your ticket!"

"So I surmised," I say dryly, but despite my attitude, her buoyancy is infectious.

"Stop being a big ol' stick in the mud," she says. "Show me where this fancy restaurant is."

We walk across the atrium to a side hall that leads to the interior entrance of the restaurant. We pass a large statue of an ancient tribal woman, tall and proud, her face and breasts painted with colorful symbols.

Vivienne stops. "Oh, I love her," she says. She

traces her own face where the lines and dots cover the woman. When her fingers cut across the top of her dress, my eyes go with them. The swell of her cleavage makes my groin tighten, and I can picture the paint on her skin.

"I would cosplay the hell out of that," she says.

I'm already visualizing undressing her and brushing color over her naked body when I realize I haven't had such a strong reaction to a woman in a long time. Something about her is so happy and bright. It's irresistible, like a childhood crush.

"We should get inside," I tell her, and lead her toward the glass door of the restaurant.

But she looks back again at the statue as we walk. And the vision of her with that paint is obviously on both of our minds.

9: Vivienne

Holy hell, this place is unbelievable.

When a fancy dude in a black vest seats us at a table, a waiter is already there. "I'll alert the chef to your arrival," he says.

I sit down, and he picks up the cloth napkin folded into the shape of a swan. Before I can ask what he's doing, he snaps it smartly and slides it across my lap.

"Be careful," I say. "Where I come from, getting that close to my business means we're betrothed."

The waiter looks up at me, shock on his face.

I laugh. "I'm just teasing." I turn to Mitch. So crazy that I spotted him in the atrium. Or maybe not, since I memorized literally every picture of him on Google. "Did you get an aperitif?"

I know I'm not impressing him, but at least I'm not totally embarrassingly unaware of how fancy schmancy restaurants like this work.

"I don't generally drink at lunch," Mitch says.

God, he's dry as a bone.

"You're going to make me drink alone?" I ask with a smile and a head tilt. If this one can be loosened up, I'm the girl for the job.

Mitch frowns a little. I think I'm getting to him. "Of course not."

"Shall I bring you both the Raki then?" the waiter asks.

"You ordered Raki as an aperitif?" Mitch asks. His eyebrows lift.

I lean forward. "It is bad?" I ask. "It's not monkey piss or anything, is it?"

And with that, it happens. Mitch Roberts cracks a smile.

The waiter looks back and forth between us. "I'm quite sure we wouldn't serve something like that," he says.

"Then why is Mitch here so amused?" I ask. My face heats up a little.

"Bring two," Mitch instructs.

The waiter nods, more than happy to escape.

"You would tell me if it's bad, right?" I ask.

"Sometimes these fancy places serve brains and entrails and all kinds of crazy things."

"No, no," Mitch says. "In fact, it's the national drink of Turkey."

I sit back a little. "It can't be that terrible then."

"Have you ever drunk absinthe?" he asks.

"You mean the stuff that made Ewan McGregor hallucinate in *Moulin Rouge*?"

And there it is again. That smile. Two-fer. I feel quite pleased since *Time* magazine called Mitch Roberts "The Most Serious Man in Venture Capital."

Sam called him "Rich Mitch," and I'm trying to scrub that from my brain now that I'm here in case I accidentally say it myself.

"I'm not familiar with that movie," Mitch says. "But absinthe today is not quite the hallucinogen it once was. It has a similar flavor to Raki. That's why I asked."

"My daddy made me drink tequila with a worm to try to scare me off liquor," I say. "I'm sure I can handle it."

"Did it work?"

"No way. I have the alcohol tolerance of a whale." My face flushes when I realize I've compared myself to a pale, blubbery animal. I really don't want that picture in his head.

But the amusement in Mitch's eyes is worth any self-deprecation. Besides, I'm good at making fun of myself. I like everyone to have a good time, and nobody can cut me down if I've already used up all the best material.

A different waiter arrives with two shots of clear liquid and two glasses filled to the brim with ice.

I have no idea what I'm doing. I smile as a shot and a glass are set in front of us both.

"Shall I prepare the Raki for you?" the waiter asks.

"Please," I say airily, as if I'm offended he thought I should do it myself.

He picks up the shot and dumps it into the ice. The liquid instantly clouds up, like a storm has rolled in.

"What in the world?" I ask, picking it up.

"Lovely, isn't it?" Mitch says. He waits for his to be poured, then holds up his glass. "To chemistry."

I raise my eyebrows at that. Maybe the cold fish is warming up. "To chemistry," I say and clink my shot against his.

I lift it to my nose and instantly pull it away. "Oh God, what is that? It smells like licorice! I hate licorice!"

Mitch cracks one more glorious smile. "Many

people agree. When it's ice cold, it takes the bite out of the flavor." He takes his glass to his lips and downs it quickly.

I sure hope so. Rich Mitch shot his like he was belly up to the bar at a bachelor party, so what the hell.

I drink quickly, holding the ice back with my teeth as the liquid pours down.

I sputter a little. The coldness takes the initial taste away, but afterward the back of my throat tastes like bad candy.

The waiter instantly sets two goblets of water on the table. I snatch one and gulp, trying to wash the awfulness out.

When I set the cup down, I say, "Okay, done it, checked off my list, and never again."

Mitch laughs. Ha. A laugh! Look at me go.

"The presentation here left a little to be desired," he says. "Ideally, the shot is chilled without being poured over ice." He looks around. "A Mediterranean place would get it right. Not sure why it's on the menu here, frankly."

"I guess I should have picked the champagne," I say. Or, I guess, Googled what Raki was. It sounded naughty, like a combination of racy and naked.

"Easily remedied." He signals the waiter again

and requests something in French.

I am so dang outclassed.

But I can fake it with the best of them.

Before the man can return with the champagne, a metal tray with ice arrives. This preordering thing is definitely efficient. Too bad. I'd like a little more time with Mitch.

It's the oysters. Six glorious half shells filled with the pearl gray meat in a glistening sauce. This waiter sets a small plate and a tiny fork in front of each of us.

This, I know. I don't get oysters often, as I'm sort of picky about where I eat them. But this is about as good as it gets.

I slide one of them onto my plate. Mitch folds his hands together and watches.

"What, you're not going to have one?" I ask.

"Raw oysters are not my favorite," he says.

"Huh." I slide the fork beneath the meat to make sure it's well detached from the shell. This is a fancy place so they probably already did it, but you never know. "I'm not sure we can be friends then," I say.

He watches me as I lift the shell and slide the oyster into my mouth. I swallow deeply and close my eyes. This is the pinnacle of oyster. Unbelievable.

I set down the empty shell. "Never mind," I say. "I'm not interested in sharing." I greedily pull a second shell to me.

"Glad you like them." He sits back and continues to watch me.

I have zero shame about knocking back the whole plate. I will never get to eat at this place again, what with its one-year waiting list and lack of prices. I have no idea what any of this costs.

Rich Mitch doesn't seem to care. Probably this is a business expense for him.

The champagne arrives. Despite this being lunch on a work day, I'm feeling decadent. The waiter opens the bottle with a satisfying pop and pours two flutes. A soft white cloud lifts from the glasses and quickly dissipates. Glorious.

"This is the best day ever," I say, lifting the glass.

Mitch has the politeness to lift his as well. The two flutes clink like a tiny bell ringing.

I never want this lunch to end.

But Mitch settles back in his chair after a single sip, eyes on me. "So what is this screening process?" he asks.

I realize the cards are in my favor. I could make the screening as complicated as I want. Dinner. Photographs. Two meetings. My eyes graze his suit. Bonus activity.

Oh, I'm terrible. And chicken. I won't do it. I like

my men willing, not tricked.

More or less. I can be as coy and flirty as I like.

I sit up a little straighter. "I have to verify that you don't make a living in some unsavory way, that you're mentally stable, and that you seem like a good fit. The clients are very high profile." I reach down to tug the application from my bag.

"You couldn't just send that over?" he asks.

"I have to be sure you are who you say you are," I say, flipping pages. "And I have to send in a picture I've taken myself."

He nods. "That's a lot of hoops to jump through."

"Oh, it's not so terrible. I just have to make sure I know who you are. It's about protection and privacy."

I pass the paperwork to him. "You can email that to me later. I'll just need to see your passport and snap an original picture."

I take out a phone.

"Oh, let's not do that here," he says. "Perhaps a little later."

Several other people in the restaurant are staring at me and my phone. I realize not a single person has theirs out, not even the people eating alone.

I tuck it back in my purse. "Is there some rule

against it?" I ask in a whisper.

"Privacy," he says. "This is a very exclusive place. People don't want to be Instagrammed."

"Oh," I say. I hadn't read anything about that when I looked the place up.

"For a while they collected phones at the entrance, but there was a little revolt," Mitch says. "Smart watches are allowed but they got out of range."

I pick up my champagne and gulp a little. My face is flaming. I hate not knowing important things. I really hate embarrassing myself, unless, of course, I did it on purpose.

"You checked out all right on my search," I say, my tone definitely more businesslike now. "Once I get the application back and I have a photo, you should be good to book. I didn't get the itinerary from your secretary."

"It's a few weeks away. Ten days to Cuba and Grand Cayman, I believe," he says.

I almost spit my drink. That's the same one my bull rider asked for.

"It should have space," I say. "I just checked it yesterday."

"Good," he says.

The next course comes. My lasagna. Mitch has a

rather sad looking salad, all nuts, seeds, and lettuce.

"I had a guinea pig once who ate more than you," I say. My fork slides through the tender noodles, sauce, and cheese like a dream.

"This is my second lunch today," he says.

"Oh, right." I take the first bite and almost swoon. It's like Christmas in my mouth. I can't contain my groan.

Mitch pauses with his fork suspended, a leaf of lettuce clinging for its life. "That good, huh?"

I nod. Best. Lunch. Ever.

We're quiet for a moment while I tackle it. I would die for leftovers, but La Traviata seems to believe in cute portions, so I'm able to finish off the square pretty handily.

Still, it's amazing.

I give Mitch props for not checking his watch even once. I'm taking up his day big time, with three courses plus drinks.

"You missed out," I say as the waiter whisks our plates away.

"I've had it," he says. "It's quite good."

I lean forward. "What does Mitch Roberts really love?"

He gives a wry smile, swirling champagne in his glass. "My work. A few of the companies are really close to my heart."

"Companies? Because of the people?"

"One of them makes heartbeat bears."

"That sounds creepy."

Another small smile. "You can record a heartbeat on a small device and place it inside the bear. When you squeeze it, it makes the sound."

This wasn't what I expected. "Why would people do that?"

"Oh, the biggest market is expecting mothers. They record their unborn baby's heartbeat to share with others. And some record their own heartbeat so the baby can hear something familiar when it sleeps in a crib."

"That's super sweet," I say. "Is that why it is dear to your heart?"

"There are lots of new markets for it. Deploying soldiers do it for those they are leaving behind. We've had some people record the heartbeats of loved ones who have terminal illnesses."

His face is calm and a little passive as he says all this emotional stuff.

But I'm not fooled.

"You wouldn't bring this up unless it was on your mind," I say. "What's going on in Mitch Roberts's world?"

He shakes his head as if he's not going to answer that.

But I'm not letting him off the hook. "You can tell me. I'm only holding the fate of your cruise in my hands."

One eyebrow lifts at that. "Are you blackmailing me?"

"Maybe just a little. Low stakes, you know."

His eyes bore into me, but I hold fast. I'm not intimidated by a big-shot billionaire. And I'll never see him again after today. So why not?

"My sister is in South Africa right now, not the most peaceful of countries," he says. "My mother died ten years ago. I'm a little short on family."

"I'm sorry," I say quickly. This is pretty personal. "Do you wish you had your mother's heartbeat?"

"Oh no. It's just that I can see the sentimental value of it. And I'm pleased to be able to keep the company afloat. Several who have tried this model have failed."

"But you won't. You're too good."

"Well, I can absorb the loss. But it's expanding. And it's a fine idea to help people keep some small proof that someone they love existed. Something tangible. Something uniquely theirs." His eyes look past me then, out at the huge windows with the curtains pulled back. The ocean sparkles through the glass.

I want to take his hand or something, but I know that is way beyond what's acceptable here.

The waiter brings my torte. I nod my thanks.

Mitch clears his throat and examines the dessert. It's chocolate, layered with cream and topped with powdered sugar and a perfect red strawberry. "Looks good," he says.

Before I can chicken out, I slip a bite on my fork and hold it across the table to him. "You must try a bite of this after that terrible seed salad."

This unnerves him a bit. I can tell because his eyes shift to the left and the right, as if concerned someone is watching.

"Nobody cares," I say. "It's just a cute girl feeding a handsome man a bite of chocolate."

His eyes meet mine over the hovering fork. "Nothing is ever that simple," he says.

"Actually, everything is that simple," I say. "It's people who make it complicated." I move the fork an inch closer. "Now eat it."

I guess my command gets to him, because he parts his lips.

The fork slides inside his mouth, and there go the lady bits again. Sparkity spark. He's been so stern, so serious, that I hadn't really taken in that mouth. It closes around the fork, and as I pull it back, the friction of it slipping out gives me a little shiver.

He swallows and licks his lips. "You were right. It is delicious." His eyes are still on mine.

Now I'm caught. The stiffness has fallen away and he's like any man, sitting across from me, full of possibility.

I take the fork and slide it into my own mouth, not even getting a bite. Just letting the warmth of the metal from his lips touch my tongue.

His eyebrow lifts again. I've surprised him. He didn't expect the curvy travel agent to proposition him.

The tension sits between us, then I let it break, looking back at the torte and taking a hefty bite.

I have to close my eyes again. It's too good.

"You're going to have to promise to get me a reservation here again sometime," I say. "I can't get one on my own."

When I open my eyes, his gaze is on my mouth and the fork.

I think I might have his attention now.

10: Mitch the Billionaire

This woman is something else.

She's clearly not used to places like this. And she obviously used her position to her advantage to get a lunch from me.

But damn it, if I can't keep my eyes off her.

She has this spark I rarely see. A vivaciousness.

I'll admit it, I'm smitten.

She works on the torte with such happy delight that it's tough to keep from smiling at her.

Except I have at least three regular business contacts in this restaurant right now and appearances to keep.

There's no telling what they think of this girl. She's obviously not someone I ordinarily do business with. Too colorful and excited.

Probably they assumed a niece or a childhood friend.

Right up until she fed me chocolate.

She pushes the plate away. "I can't possibly eat it all," she says. "Way too rich." Her face pinks up at that, and I wonder why.

The pages sit next to my glass and I glance at them. It all seems pretty straightforward. I'm not fond of the extra steps in taking this cruise, but I don't mind that it put me in contact with Vivienne. She's been the most entertaining lunch date I have had in a long time.

Bonnie knows if I don't arrive by a certain time to reschedule my day. I haven't checked the time, but I'm quite sure I've missed my 1:30 already and might be closing in on the 2:00.

But I'm not going to rush.

As unexpected as it is, I'm interested in her.

The waiter brings another glass, this one a crystal highball glass with amber liquid. She's really quite outdone herself for a lunch.

"What is this?" I ask.

"Brandy," she says, lifting the glass for a sniff. "It's got the best aroma."

She takes a sip. "Oh, and it's amazing."

I remember the feel of the fork sliding out of my

mouth and the jolt of watching her take it inside hers. Definitely not a shy one.

I want to feel like that again. The electric charge is intoxicating and rare. I can't remember when I last experienced it.

I extend a hand. "May I?" I ask.

"Sure," she says and passes it over.

The sweet woodsy scent of good brandy wafts up as it reaches my nose. I hold up the glass. There's a faint imprint of her rosy lipstick on the crystal.

"I like this color on you," I say, eyes on the glass.

"Passion Pink," she says.

"I bet." I lift the glass, carefully turning it so that the lipstick print aligns with my mouth.

Vivienne sucks in a quick breath as I drink. She noticed.

The charge comes again, a slow burn that lights from within. When I look at her, she has pressed her hands to her belly.

She feels it.

My cock stirs now. Perhaps it would be wise to go ahead and move this forward. Get on with it, take her, and put her from my mind.

I think ahead to my afternoon. Can I clear it or should I ask her to dinner?

She gazes at me with something akin to fondness.

No, not dinner. That would be too much and might make her cling. I need a one and done. If she's up for it.

"Shall we go to my office so we can get the photo out of the way?" I ask.

She nods, her eyes drifting from my face to my shoulders, then down to the edge of the table. Yes, she feels it. I'll present an opportunity, see if she'll bite.

I can be persuasive.

I stand and hurry to her chair to pull it back. This gives me a generous view of her cleavage, and I stir a little harder. I'll be quite persuasive, actually.

The staff know where to send the bill. I pick up the stack of papers and lead Vivienne to the door. She doesn't take my arm like she did the first time. I fear I've made her self-conscious after the phone incident.

As we make our way across the atrium, I'm aware of every swish of her skirt, the gentle sway of her breasts, how her hair bounces in its little curls in the back. She reminds me of a vintage poster, the perfectly coiffed roll above her forehead, and the dress that fits so exactly at the torso then flares out at the knees.

I turn her away from the main concourse to the back hall, where a private elevator is available. I don't take it often, considering it pretentious, but it serves my purpose today.

"What's this?" she asks as we go down the quiet hall.

"The executive elevator," I say.

"Oh!"

We approach the elevator and I swipe a card to open the doors. Inside, the walls are mirrors and the floor is carpeted.

"I love getting to see behind the scenes," she says.

"I loved having lunch with someone as interesting and lovely as yourself," I say.

Her eyes flit up to me then. "I got the impression that your secretary felt this was a terrible bother that would disrupt your schedule."

I look down at her big brown eyes. Her lashes are a mile long. The faint remains of her Passion Pink lipstick draw me like a glass of water on a hot day.

The elevator slowly rises. She sways a little, and I take it as an opportunity to touch her waist to steady her.

She sucks in a breath. Her eyes are still on me, and I don't take mine off her. The chemistry swirling around us is almost as visible as the vapor off the champagne.

"How private is your office?" she asks. "For the picture, I mean."

"Very," I say.

She slips her hand into mine, and the contact is like an electric charge. I'm raging beneath my control. It feels so clandestine, like we're two secret lovers plotting a rendezvous.

The elevator opens on my floor. It's another private hallway. I can take us through a side entrance and only encounter a few data entry personnel.

I unlock the door. The cubicles here are quiet, keyboards clicking. A few people look up but don't seem to notice me holding Vivienne's hand. It's hard to really see us with all the walls.

I shouldn't care. I'm their boss. And single. There is nothing scandalous here.

My card keys us through another side door to the conference room adjacent to my office. Vivienne slows down, admiring the leather swivel chairs, running her fingers along the glossy wood table. "It's beautiful," she says.

I suppose it is, taking it in from her perspective. The room exudes opulence and power, designed to make investors feel confidence in my company.

We pass through. Bonnie is not at her desk, probably still watching the cat.

Oh. The cat. I pause. I guess it's fine.

It doesn't matter. I don't even know what's going to happen. Possibly nothing.

I open the door to my office, and Bonnie looks up. She's typing on her laptop next to Belle's red throne.

"She's so pretty!" Vivienne gasps, breaking away to approach the cat. "You bring your pet to work!"

"Technically, she's my sister's," I say.

Bonnie glances over at Vivienne, then at me. "What about your two o'clock?" she asks.

"Reschedule," I say. "And my three."

Bonnie's mouth drops open. "That's the Japanese contingent."

"Move them to four and send four to tomorrow."

She nods and glances back over at the girl. "Some screening," she says.

"It's...involved," I say.

She tucks her laptop under her arm and heads out. When the door is closed, I softly lock it.

Vivienne looks up. She's kneeling in front of Belle, stroking her soft fur. "Have you always kept your kitty here?"

"Belle hasn't been feeling well, so I keep an eye on her."

"That's very involved of you," Vivienne says. "My mom wouldn't let our kitties in the house."

"She belonged to my mother," I say before I can catch myself.

This gets Vivienne's attention. Her hand slows to rest on Belle's back. "So she's special."

"Belle means the world to my sister. I won't let anything happen to her."

Vivienne stands up. "I think that is amazing and beautiful." She fiddles with the edge of her skirt. "I guess I should get that picture."

I sense she might take it and leave.

And I don't want her to leave.

"I thought you should try a different brandy than the one at lunch," I say smoothly as I head to a cabinet near my desk. "That one was good, but nothing like this." I pause, looking back at her. "If you're up for it."

She watches me. "Mitch Roberts, are you trying to get me drunk in your private office, when you just locked the door? In the middle of the day?"

Oh, this girl. She says what she means.

"Is that a yes?" I ask.

"Only if that's a yes from you."

Damn. Vivienne is something. I think of all the uptight stoic women who seem to mostly tolerate me for my money and wonder where Vivienne has been all my life.

I take a little risk. "I'm pretty sure I couldn't say no to you for anything." I open the compartment and take two glasses from the rack.

She wanders over to look in. "That's a lot of booze for a business office. My boss gets mad if we have a margarita at lunch."

Yet she had two drinks here today. Interesting.

I set the glasses on a tray and add a bottle of brandy I save for special moments.

"That looks fancy," she says. "Louis the Thirteenth?"

"It's a cognac that is over a century old," I say.

"Wow," she says. "That's crazy!"

"Very rare bottle." I uncap it carefully and decant an inch or so into each glass. "Extremely flavorful."

I recap the bottle and hand a glass to Vivienne.

"To unexpected lunches," I say, and clink her glass.

"To the unexpected," she returns.

She sips her drink and makes that lovely groaning sound again. I imagine her doing it in a different circumstance and my groin tightens.

"This is unlike anything I've ever tasted," she says. "I like the way you live."

She smiles up at me, and I have to admit, I'm caught like there are strings around me, pulling me toward her.

"You haven't tasted yours," she says, taking another cautious sip.

I lean in close. "I want to taste it on you."

Her eyes lift up to me. "Then why don't you?"

Her mouth parts softly as our lips meet. She tastes of liquor, chocolate, and champagne. I can't get enough of her, feeling the control I prize slipping as I tangle my fingers in the silky curls at the back of her neck.

My tongue explores her, warm and yielding. Her breasts press gently into my chest. We move together, connected, her body shifting against mine with agonizing closeness.

I take her glass and set it on my desk. My hands want everywhere at once — her waist, her back, her arms. My thumb grazes a nipple, and she inhales sharply. This is literally the craziest thing I've ever done, coming on so strong to someone I met only an hour ago. In my office, no less.

But her hands slide beneath my jacket and make their way up. And I'm not going to retreat now. I feel buoyant, painfully alive. She pushes my jacket off my shoulders and it falls to the floor.

My hands take both breasts at once. She's delicious and tempting, and I'm not going to back away from this need I have. She shivers from my touch, so responsive, so passionate. Her mouth seeks mine with more pressure, more depth.

I walk us to the far corner of the office to the red leather sofa. I'm going to have her, brand her as mine. I need her, the lifeblood she's giving me. I've never acted like this before, always so cautious not to upset a well-connected family or a jealous socialite.

She owes me nothing, and I don't owe her. It's the most even exchange I've encountered since I started my business.

I'm free to be hungry, demanding, to give in. I press her down onto the sofa. She begins unbuttoning my shirt, and I reach behind her for the zipper to her dress. I must see this body, all of it, touch it, taste her.

Vivienne manages to pull out my cuff links and gets the shirt off me. I lift her, unzipping the back of her dress. As she falls back to the sofa, I pull it forward and down her arms.

Her bra is pale, a creamy yellow that accents her hair. "Now there's the picture," I say gruffly.

"Take it if you like," she says. "I've worn less in public."

I've never even considered such a thing, having a

half-naked image of a woman on my phone. But I want this, of her, and so I tug my cell from my pants.

Vivienne settles back, one arm draped above her head.

The light flows in through the sheer curtains above the sofa, lighting her up. I'm no photographer, but this is glorious. I take the shot.

And I want more.

I want those glorious breasts captured for my personal pleasure.

My hands surround the cups of the bra. "May I?" I ask.

"Of course you may," she says.

I reach for the hook and slide the bra away from her body.

My cock rages now, straining in the confines of my suit pants. Her breasts are perfect, full and round with tight pink nipples.

I pick up the phone. "I would guard this image with my life."

She laughs a little. "This one only. Nothing crazier."

I lift my phone. She's still half-laughing, her beautiful mouth caught partially open, her eyes alight with amusement, when I take the shot.

God. I'm wild for her.

I toss the phone on the rug and bend down. Time to touch and taste. My mouth closes over that gorgeous nipple.

Vivienne arches up. I feel crazed, wanting every inch of her, my hands running down her body, mouth taking in one breast then the other, over and over again.

She unbuckles my pants, pushing down the zipper and freeing my cock so that it rests against her belly.

I grasp the dress and push it all the way down and away. Now she has panties, little pale yellow ones with a bow in front. I make my way down and press a kiss onto that bow.

There is no stopping us now.

11: Vivienne

Holy oysters on a half shell, I'm nearly naked in a billionaire's office.

It's not that I don't get in situations like this. I do all the time.

It's just usually a pickup truck or a motel or somebody's bedroom with roommates watching football down the hall.

This time I've drunk brandy that probably costs a month's rent. Or two. Who knows with these rich people.

And I let him take pictures.

Which, let's be real, isn't the first time.

And he's killing me. His chest is lean and has the sort of muscles you'd expect on a dancer, wiry and strong. Probably all those seed salads.

And he's a greedy bugger, eating me up like he wants *me* for lunch.

His mouth is down low, and I can feel the heat of his breath in amazing places. His fingers curl around the lacy edge, and down the panties go, over my thighs, past my knees, then flying across the coffee table.

The leather feels amazing, warm and luxurious, heated up by my skin.

The light is bright through the window. I'm at the highest floor of the building and definitely on top of the world.

His mouth lands down there, and I hold on to the cushions. His hands lift my hips up to him, and holy hell, he knows what he's doing.

He finds that little nub and works it like it's his personal plaything. Which right now, it is.

I can't help but rock against him, flooded with pleasure. He can really tease it out, make it last, pulling back and evening me out before I cross over the edge.

I'm ready to grab his head and hold him hostage. But he knows, he gets it. When he takes it up that last notch, I'm gone, sailing, my body pulsing, headed right into the light.

Take me now, Jesus, as I'm ready to for heaven, full up on fancy food and old brandy and this orgasm that he's stringing out, keeping going, how is he doing that?

I want to scream but it's his office and God, I have to find some decency in me. He finally lets me down and starts kissing his way across my belly. I relax into the cushions and try to pull myself together. I glance across the room and spot Belle snoozing on her throne. She couldn't care less what we're up to.

I turn back to Mitch. He has a devilish look in his eye. He stands to kick off his shoes and drop his pants and boxers.

My eyes go straight to what I'm anxious to see, and I'm not disappointed. Long and perfectly straight, uncut and aimed right at me. He walks away for a moment, and I wonder what he's up to. He opens a drawer and comes back with a glass of brandy and a condom.

"Interesting combination," I tell him. "Is sipping booze from latex something the rich folk do?"

He cracks a smile. "You say the most unexpected things."

He sets the condom down and leans over me with the glass. "I tasted this on your lips, but I want to see what other parts of you do to the flavor."

His finger dips into the liquor, then spreads it across my nipple.

His mouth goes down, and I drop my head back. This is just too much fun.

My belly button is next. He flicks his tongue inside.

"You're crazy," I say.

"We both are," he says. "Now turn over."

"Oh!" I pull my legs close and roll over, moving to hands and knees.

His cold finger spreads booze along my spine. His mouth follows, warm and wet.

Damn, that's sexy.

The condom wrapper rustles and I turn to look.

Mitch is behind me, sliding the condom over his glorious cock. Then his hands come to my back.

I let my head fall forward as he works along my shoulders and neck, massaging anything tense. When I'm good and relaxed, he moves back down, holding my hips.

There's a pause, then he slams into me with such incredible force I'm almost knocked forward. I let out a little squeal. He has a solid grip, and as soon as I'm ready for the next one, I hold tight and let him have his way with me.

It's hot and hard and makes me feel light-headed, like I'm on an amusement park ride. I find myself gasping, lighting bolts charging through me like a thunderstorm.

Every thrust pushes me up the stairway to heaven. I'm gonna be calling to Jesus twice on the same sofa.

Mitch braces himself on one arm and reaches around me with the other. His fingers find my clit, and God, here we go again.

I'm wrung out and hot and want to beg for it. But he's got stamina and style, and just when I start to think about what we're doing, he shifts, and I lose my mind again. He presses me forward over the arm of the sofa, taking the weight off my arms.

It's bliss, and I focus only on the bursting sensation of his cock riding in and out of my body. Luxurious leather. The old-world smell of his office. I pretend for a moment I'm the deadly gorgeous lover of this man of wealth and power.

I mean, I am, a little, but for real, for more than once. I imagine I could saunter in and pour a glass of one-hundred-year-old cognac and knock it back like a dollar shot without care.

Then lift my leg to land my thousand-dollar Louboutin stiletto on his desk, my leather skirt parting, showing off crotchless panties.

Oh, the fantasy during the fantasy.

But then I'm back, and he's speeding up, and

God, I'm in the moment, stars colliding everywhere, whole constellations going up in smoke as the white-hot orgasm starts to burst through my body.

"Shit, shit, shit," is my ladylike response, but I've totally lost my grip on reality, riding a cosmic high. He shudders behind me, adding his pulse to the rhythmic vibrations inside me as he comes.

I drop my head to the round arm of the sofa, completely spent. Sign my death certificate, because I'm a goner.

Mitch folds in behind me, his body heavy on mine, his lips against my ear. We breathe together for a long while, my first clue that I am not, actually, dead.

"I want to see you again," he says.

Okay, now I want to live. The Louboutins are back on the desk.

Where can I buy crotchless panties?

Oh, silly, reader, don't listen to the rantings of a dead woman. I already have three pair.

I manage to gush out an, "Okay," even though I don't do a lot of second encounters. They're usually disappointing, and I like the good ones to stand like martyrs on the sacrificial table of my life, perfect and pure.

But the perks here are just too good.

Mitch pulls away and slides from my body. He's a

half-master even after the deed. I think he might be an exception to the disappointing seconds.

Or worse, the don't-actually-call-agains.

Because I have to face facts. I'm a poor working girl with a potty mouth and a dead-end job. A couple nasty comments from one of Mitch's billionaire pals about slumming it with the chub and his jets will cool off. He'll go back to his models and Ivy League lawyer girls.

Gramma told me there would be the right man for me somewhere, and I'm a believer. But I'm also not into getting my heart crushed over and over. So the real deal will have to prove it way beyond the willingness of the average man.

I know my place.

Still, this could be fun. Guard my heart and eat very nice meals.

We pull on our clothes. I think Mitch's wildly spiked hair will do nicely for my cruise photo, but he won't do it. So I fix it for him and take the nice shot. When I review it, I see Brady's too. Oh, the bull rider.

My heart doesn't pang. It was one of those clear one and dones. The can't-do-anything-about-it variety who lives somewhere else or has some other problem.

Still nice encounters. Still fun.

Just like Mitch.

I know he said he wanted to see me again. But that doesn't mean he will.

I pet the kitty as I walk by and wait for Mitch to unlock the door.

My head is high as we pass the secretary, who watches from the corner of her eye.

The front way out is different from the side. As Mitch escorts me though these open desks, every face pops up. They don't know how long we've been in there or what we've been doing. I guess I just don't meet the expectation of his usual business guest.

"Thank you for your generous donation to our boarding school," I say as we walk through. "The orphans will enjoy the new playground."

I think I see a smile flirt on his lips as we exit the office and approach the main elevator bay. "You're something else, Ms. Carter," he says.

"I was just thinking of the poor children, Mr. Roberts," I say.

"Indeed. The children."

He wants to grin at me, I can tell. I've cracked the impassive venture capitalist. I should call *Time* magazine. They can make me Woman of the Year.

But in reality, the elevator dings and the doors open. I remind him to have his secretary send in his application so I can book the cruise.

And step inside.
And go.
We'll see if he calls again.
I'm not holding my breath.

12: Mitch the Billionaire

The day is almost at a close when I realize I don't have Vivienne's number. I've been practically useless, sneaking peeks at her naked-breasted picture while listening to endless presentations by young start-up hopefuls asking for venture capital.

"Bonnie," I say into the intercom. "Do you have the number of that travel agent who was here earlier?"

She pauses longer than is necessary for a reply. I wonder if she senses something is off, or disapproves.

Finally, she says, "I have her work number. I can patch you through."

Good enough.

I wait, drumming my fingers on the desk. It isn't quite five. Hopefully she is still in the office.

Bonnie comes back on. "Vivienne has left for the

day. Would you like to speak to her supervisor Janet Fitch?"

The woman who hates margaritas at lunch.

"No, no," I say, not quite getting the dark note out of my voice.

"Is there something about the cruise booking I can do? I sent her the application and a scan of your passport."

"Did she reply?" I'm oddly concerned she didn't make it back somehow. That there was a car accident or she was accosted on the street. My heart rate quickens as I picture her being attacked by a stranger.

I have to pull myself together. It's ridiculous. I just met her.

"Yes, she thanked me for being prompt."

Well, okay. She's fine, I suppose.

"Give me the number. I'll try myself tomorrow."

She rattles off the digits and I jot them on a notepad. I'd rather cut Bonnie out of the communication anyway.

"Thank you," I say. "Good night."

"You haven't forgotten the dinner meeting, right?" she asks. "The Hong Kong investors? They're pretty insistent."

I had, actually. But I say, "Of course not."

"You wanted me to be there to help the

translators."

Right. "Yes, are you staying through?"

"I don't have time to go home and come back," she says.

"Very well, we'll leave together. At seven?" I glance at the electronic calendar and see that indeed, I had forgotten that meeting. The three appointments I blew off today for Vivienne are outlined in red.

Worth it.

"I'll be out here," she says.

I shut off the line and pull out my phone. There Vivienne is again, pooled in sunlight, the first one serene and covered. The second one laughing, her breasts tempting me sorely.

I haven't mooned over a woman like this since I was fourteen years old.

Ridiculous.

I should delete the images. Forget about her. She's going to be bad for business. A distraction.

But I can't. I'm dying to touch her again. Do everything. I can still hear her cries ringing on the walls.

"What do I do, Belle?" I ask the cat.

She turns to me impassively and meows. Even she's a little perkier today. A vet tech is coming for her shortly, to babysit and make sure she's doing well while I am at dinner.

Such a spoiled kitty.

I turn to my computer. I can't call Vivienne tonight, and I'm stuck in this meeting anyway.

Tomorrow.

Tomorrow I'll see her again.

I'll make sure of it.

13: Vivienne

I realize when I'm halfway through a pint of Ben & Jerry's after dinner (okay, busted, the ice cream *is* my dinner) that Mitch doesn't have my cell phone number, and I don't have his.

I'm not going to call that snooty secretary. She already sent in his application anyway. All the numbers were for his business. I already checked. I forwarded the payment portal for when he's approved. Of course he will be.

I laugh to think about both Brady and Mitch on the same boat. There are thirty cabins and a full crew. It's not likely they'll sit at the same table and figure out they banged the same bimbo.

But honestly, the thought of that very scenario makes me less enthusiastic about the billionaire. What if he's taking someone else on the trip?

And Brady. He's like, gone.

Ugh. I really shouldn't sleep with clients. I know where they're going.

And I'm just where they've been.

The next day at work is pure drudgery. Nobody calls. Not the secretary or Mitch. And I know my work number is all over the paperwork he had.

Sam sends me sympathetic looks as I mope through the work hours.

I stay strong right up until 4:30. He'll be going home soon. Maybe I can fake my way through a phone call and get to him.

The application gives me the general information number for his company. I call it and ask for Mitch Roberts. I'm sent to another girl who definitely isn't his secretary. She's way too young and perky. I picture a cute administrative assistant bent over his red sofa and feel a major pang of jealousy.

"Mr. Roberts isn't available. May I take a message for him?" she asks.

"Is his secretary there? This is about his upcoming travel," I say.

"You mean his trip to Hong Kong? He and Bonnie aren't expected back until next week."

Hong Kong? He's out of the country?

"No, his cruise. It's fine. I can speak with them when they are back." I hang up.

He's in Hong Kong.

I check the time difference. It's big. It would make it hard to call.

If that's it.

He didn't mention the trip yesterday.

Of course, we didn't do a lot of chitchat.

Sam looks over at me. She's putting on her sweater to head home. "It's Friday night! You want to go get a drink?" she asks. "Pick up a new guy?" She's happy being my wing man, especially if I've done a bunch of failed auditions and need to get my numbers up.

Or like now, when I'm blue.

Case in point number eight: I'm often blue. My life is this crazy pendulum between elation and despair.

I shake my head. "Going to take it easy," I say.

"You could sing," she says. "It's karaoke o'clock somewhere."

That girl knows me.

And it's true. Even if it's not open mic at FreakEasy, there's tons of other lesser places. Singing will make me feel better. Singing is the best of everything.

In the end, Sam convinces me to go to some family-friendly karaoke at a restaurant. I wind up singing Disney Princess ballads to a birthday party, and that doesn't feel too bad. Those adorable little girls treat me like a star, bringing me a sprinkle-studded cupcake and insisting on pictures.

I go to bed without feeling like I've tried to rebound on a one-night stand, which really is ridiculous. By definition, I shouldn't need to rebound on the rebound of the rebound. But these last two have been pretty different from all that came before. The bull rider and the billionaire. Sounds like a movie title.

It's possible I'm getting old or my ovaries are ready to sow *their* oats. Or eggs. Or whatever. But maybe seventy-three is enough.

It'll be a long weekend. I can go in to the travel agency on Saturday if I want. There's a weekend crew, but my desk is mine and I'm allowed to pick up clients any day the store front is open. Which is to say, every day except Sunday.

But with two Blue Sapphire Yacht commissions coming in as soon as the final payments are made, I'm feeling complacent. I'll be lazy, maybe practice a new number for FreakEasy. Watch for any open auditions.

And just be me for a couple days. Boyless me.

14: Vivienne

Monday rolls around as it does.

There's no voice mail for me, no scribbled messages from the agents there on Saturday.

Fine.

I examine the Hong Kong time zone. It's 9 a.m. here. So 11 p.m. there. Okay, maybe open of business is too late for him to call. But when I get off at 4 it will be…6 a.m. there.

Shoot. Unless he's a late nighter or an early riser, my work hours are while he sleeps.

So maybe it's just timing.

Or maybe Billionaire was a dud.

It's too hard to think about it, so I shove it from my mind. None of the other one-timers got to me like this. I need to buck the hell up.

Around lunch, I get a notification from Blue Sapphire Yachts that both of my applicants were approved and to forward their chosen itineraries at my earliest convenience. I send along the payment portal and links to Brady and Mitch so they can confirm their dates, make the deposit, and then I can enter them into the ship's cabin assignment system.

When I check availability, I see the cruise they want is quickly filling up. Dang. I want to make sure they get on it. But until they confirm, the system won't give me an authorization to hold a cabin for them. It's a clunky system designed to ensure a booking is absolutely final. Only one of the ten authorized agencies can be logged in at a time to avoid booking errors. If someone walks away without closing the screen, you can get locked out for hours.

But the commissions are amazing, so you put up with it.

Janet takes a call in the back, and Sam and I try to look busy. I fuss with a mirror, poking at the pin curls I attempted. I've decided vintage hairstyles are the look for me, since I've already got a bod that fits better in a halter dress.

I almost get seven years of bad luck when Janet suddenly speaks behind me. I fumble with the mirror and manage to keep it from falling to the floor.

"Pick up line two," she says.

My heart hammers. Is it Mitch finally?

"Who is it?"

"Somebody who will only book with you." Her voice is irritated. As manager, she's probably noticed I got two Sapphires, and now somebody is calling just me.

I wait for her to walk back. Sam's staring right at me. She's dying to know if it's the billionaire too.

I pick up the receiver and punch the line button. "Hello?"

"Is this Vivienne Carter?" a deep voice asks.

But it is not Mitch's voice.

I shake my head at Sam, who deflates a little.

Me too, girlfriend.

"Yes, I'm Vivienne."

"This is Bart Jacoby. I've been looking you up on the internet."

My heart hammers. Is he a music executive? Or have I finally been busted messing with the wrong man? I check for wedding rings, I swear I do!

"How can I help you?" I ask, my voice wavering.

"This is an odd request. It will require a personal touch."

Now, I think he's a stalker.

"Our agency is open if you want to come by," I

say, quickly turning to the computer and typing in "Bart Jacoby."

"I'm out of the country," he says. "But my son happens to be in Miami at the moment."

Is he setting me up with his son?

Now, I think there must be some web site equivalent of the bathroom wall, and my name and number has been posted under "Easy."

Which, to be honest, is fair.

But still. I picture some teen boy needing to become a man. So his father is bringing him to me like fathers did with their sons in brothels of old.

Ye olde Vivienne brothel.

The search results come up. Holy guacamole.

Bart Jacoby is a senator.

A very powerful senator.

So is one of his sons. Randall Jacoby.

Is this the son? He doesn't look too bad.

But also, married. I scroll through a dozen wedding shots.

"You still there?" he asks.

"Yes. What exactly do you need from me, Mr. Jacoby?"

He sighs. "There's a cruise I want my son to go on. I'm hoping to convince him not to re-enlist."

"The military?" I look at the pictures of the son.

He doesn't look military in his fancy suit and perfect hair.

"He's completed his contract as a Navy SEAL, which made me very proud, but he's doing it for all the wrong reasons. I need him to meet some important people on this cruise, people who can convince him that it's time for him to move his public service into the political arena."

This dude is a piece of work.

"I'm sorry, sir, but if he's a SEAL, he's got to be what — late twenties? Can't he figure this out on his own?"

Sam gives me a "what the hell" look. I shrug.

"I certainly can't convince him, but I believe this person can. I just need him on that boat. I will triple your commission."

Damn. That's a lot of money.

"What if he doesn't go? I don't get anything."

My breath holds, waiting to see what Bart Jacoby will say.

"You get half a commission just for trying."

How does he want me to try? My face pinks up. Seduce him into going?

I turn back to the computer. "What is your son's name?" I ask.

"Do we have a deal?" he asks.

I hesitate. If this guy is a SEAL, then he's at least in shape. And there's a code of conduct involved. He could be aggressive, though. Although picturing some sexy cut dude ordering me around actually stirs the juices a little.

"Yes," I say. "What did you have in mind?"

Dear old Dad gives me the name of the hotel where his son John is staying. He'll arrange the meeting tomorrow night in the downstairs bar.

"Be persuasive," he says. "I have confidence in you."

"What made you pick me?" I ask. "You were talking to my manager before."

"When I logged into Blue Sapphire Yachts, you are now the top-rated agent," he says. "Your reviews are stellar. I believe one said, 'If I could take her with me, I'd never set foot on land again.'"

My heart hammers. Did Mitch do that? Or Brady?

"Wow," I say. "I didn't know they reviewed us."

"I take a lot of Blue Sapphire Yachts," he says. "I have perks."

"Okay," I say. "I'll do my best."

"Forward me the payment portal, and I'll send the half-commission now," he says. "If he books and gets on the boat, I'll forward the rest."

"All right." I take down his email and end the call.

Sam stands up. "What was that?"

"Just another Sapphire booking."

She pushes my arm. "You said you were going to give the next one to me!"

"Sorry," I say. "He would only work with me. Turned Janet down flat. I'll send you the next one, I promise."

She crosses her arms. "Sounds like this one is going to be interesting. You're meeting his son?"

I nod. "Yeah. It's worth a triple commission —" I see Janet raise her head and I lower my voice. "I get triple if he gets on the boat. I'm supposed to convince him."

Sam shakes her head. "Another notch on the lipstick case ahead," she says.

Huh. Maybe. "He might be married or have a girlfriend."

"True," she says. "But if he's just coming off military duty, maybe not."

I don't know that much about SEALs. We spend some time looking up their tour of duty. We search for John Jacoby but find nothing except a family photo when he was twelve and Dad was running for senate.

"I don't think he's that little boy anymore," Sam says.

I stare at the kid, brown hair falling over his eyes, frowning between his older brother and a younger sister. His mother has her hands on his shoulders, as if he might take off running if she didn't keep him in place.

Yeah, he looks like a rebel. Not doing Daddy's bidding. I don't think I'm going to see that triple commission. But it looks like fun and definitely takes my mind off the deadbeat billionaire.

Now to find the right dress for the meeting.

My email dings and Daddio has made good on his word. A hefty three figures just got sent. I turn to Sam. "It's lunch time. Let's go shopping."

15: John the SEAL

Only three damn days into my break between contracts, and dear old Dad is already planning my exit strategy. The only thing I'm up for this morning is to parlay this anger into a killer workout.

The hotel gym leaves a lot to be desired. No free weights. All universal bullshit. The belt is loose on two of the treadmills, and this twiggy bottle blond I could break like a stick stays on the good one for literally hours.

The elliptical works, though, and I can cycle through some pretty intense intervals on it. And I unearthed two fifty-pound sandbag weights that are perfect for caveman throws.

Still, I'll never be up for the next deployment if I drop the intensity of my workouts. I lucked out on my first team. We had missions with real-deal consequences, mostly underwater explosives. I'm not going to slack off now.

Twiggy finally touches her pristine white towel to her temple and steps off the treadmill. I need to get fourteen miles in before lunch, so I'm glad she's finally getting off it.

She flashes me a heated look as she passes. Whatever. That diamond on her finger makes her off limits, and besides, I would break her in twenty seconds.

Solitude is blissful. I can really go all out. I crank that treadmill and tear along the rolling floor like I'm on the chase.

Because next time, I might be. I've heard rumors about what could be next for my team. At the end of this break, I'm to report and get my new assignment.

If my father doesn't interfere.

This is when being in a political family sucks. My SEAL contract is up. I'm free to be a civilian. I have no intention of doing that. I'm not interested in running for office or working the lobby. I can't imagine a bigger waste of space.

But my dad has connections. Connections that could actually kill my SEAL career, if he wants to go that far.

I thought my brother Randall taking up the flag would be enough, but no, Dad thinks my military background will make me an even better candidate.

Like hell it will.

If being a SEAL has taught me anything, it's to cut through the bullshit. Only when you're facing twenty-foot waves crashing your tiny floater into jagged rock and half your platoon falls overboard do you really know who has your back.

My phone beeps, but I ignore it. It's just Dad. He's insisting I meet some lackey of his at the hotel bar tonight. "Just hear her out," he says. "She has some interesting connections that are right in line with your interests."

Right. A bunch of liars and lawyers, no doubt, not that there's any difference to me. The only thing that counts is what happens when your life is on the line. Not some ethics bill. Which shouldn't even be fucking necessary. Just have ethics, assholes. And not some gerrymandering bullshit. Just draw points from A to B. And done.

My anger really pushes me into the redline, and I max out the speed of the treadmill. Stupid lame equipment. I run flat out for half a mile, then coax it down before I end up flying into the wall.

I skip two meals and work out for six hours, just

to keep my edge. By the time dinner comes around, I'm ready to eat a house and all its occupants.

But I'm supposed to go to a bar. A bar. Like I drink during training. My father doesn't know shit about one thing that's important to me.

He sends a picture so I know how to find this girl he's forcing on me. I have to say, she isn't what I expect. She's laughing, bright hair in some sort of 1940s getup, and her rack could nurse a small country.

All right. I'll talk to that. But the minute she starts pushing me into the family business, I'm out.

I don't want to look a thing like my father or brother or their cronies, so I slide on a pair of jeans and a Navy hoodie. Add a pair of black boots, and I'm quite sure I'll stand out completely in the downstairs of this stupidly swanky hotel.

I'm only in Miami at all to do some cliff diving. Mom booked this place for me, but it's not my style whatsoever. I'd rather sleep on the beach, honestly.

The bar is dim. I look around for this girl Dad sent. She isn't sitting on any of the stools, and a quick search turns up empty at the tables.

I slide into a booth. A waitress brings a menu.

Actually the food options aren't half bad. I order the biggest burger they've got and my one vice — a soda.

The meeting time passes and still no girl. Awesome. Maybe she'll no-show and I can move on.

My food arrives, and I tear into the burger, fat and delicious. I could eat for six years. It feels good to fast and push myself, then carb back up. Everything tastes like heaven.

I'm totally focused on the task at hand when a woman pauses by my table. "John?" she asks.

I look up. It's her. She's way better in person than her photo. Her hair is a thousand curls, like a goddamn halo. She wears a black dress that makes me regret my hoodie. It molds to her body like it was made for her, flaring out at the hips, classic and very Marilyn Monroe. In fact, she's got the whole Marilyn vibe.

"That's me," I say, dropping the burger and jumping to my feet. I don't have to care about what she's saying to enjoy watching those red lips say it.

"I'm Vivienne," she says. "Your dad asked me to meet you. I think that's a first for me." She smiles and her eyes are bright and happy. I can't help but smile back.

"First for me, too," I say. "Please, sit down."

When she slides into the booth, the little light over the table brightens up the deep cleft between her breasts, and it takes a helluva lot of willpower to look away. Where did Dad find this girl?

"I'll get a waitress," I tell her, making eye contact with the woman who took my order. She hurries over.

Vivienne looks up at her, and I can take her in without her noticing. She's something else with her movie-star quality. That chest must be held up by some magical contraption because it stands at attention like a first-phase trainee.

Hell. I've been on platoon duty for twenty-two months without a stand down. I don't even see women for months at a time. She's better than the feast on my plate.

She orders a brandy.

"You should get some food," I say.

She looks down at the mostly-eaten burger. "I ate already."

The way she says it makes my cock stir. I wonder if this is what Dad intended. He sent me her picture. Surely she's not a prostitute.

"What do you do?" I ask her.

"I'm a travel agent," she says. "I book adventure packages mostly."

Now this does interest me. "Like what?"

"Jungle expeditions, cruises, desert tours, hikes, cliff diving —"

"I'm going cliff diving tomorrow."

"Really? Off the North Miami Beach?" she asks. Her finger twirls a piece of her hair.

"Yeah, is that the best?" Hell, this girl might prove useful.

"I think so," she says.

"Do you do it?"

She blushes. "Oh no. But I book them for people who are traveling here."

"Huh." I sit back. "I've done mountain climbing, rappelling, skydiving, paragliding, bungee."

"So you're a thrill seeker."

"I like to push the limits, sure." I catch her eyes. She's intrigued.

"You ever been kitesurfing?" she asks.

Now I lean forward. "No. Never heard of it."

Her brandy arrives, and she turns the glass in her hands, gazing at the amber liquid. "It's sort of a combination of surfing, paraglide, and snowboard. You can do it off the shore here, but it's way better near an ocean island like Grand Cayman."

"Really? Can you get to Cayman from here?" This sounds like gold. I always fill my time off with new shit. And this sounds good.

"You can. There's a really great cruise in a couple weeks. I could plan some extreme sports at every stop for you." She gives me a small smile and takes a sip of her drink.

And that's when it hits me. It's a setup.

"So what's in it for you?" I ask.

"It's my job!" she says with a tilt of her head. "I get a very nice commission."

I don't buy it.

"Why did my father send you here?"

"For this, actually," she says. "He wanted you to see the perks of civilian life. Sounded a little overbearing, if you ask me." She rummages through a bag and pulls out a couple brochures. "If I were you, I'd blow me off just to piss *him* off."

I pick up my burger again and take a couple bites, considering everything she's just said. Either she's smarter than anybody who's worked for my father, or she's shooting straight on this.

"How do you know my father?" I ask.

She takes a sip of her drink. "I'm the highest-rated agent for the service he uses. He was willing to pay me extra to meet with you."

Great. So she's only here for the money. I forget any concerns I had about sitting here eating while she sips a drink.

"Fine. So what else you got for an adrenaline junkie?" I ask. I'm not letting my guard down, no way. But she does seem to know her stuff.

"You ever been in underwater caves?" I ask.

I swallow. "That's classified," I say.

Her laugh is seriously the happiest sound I've heard in a year. My guard slips a little. No way she's faking all this.

"I love it," she says. "Well underwater spelunking might be just a day in the life of a Navy SEAL, but this one has bioluminescence. The water glows blue. It's incredible."

I'm definitely intrigued. "Have you been there?"

She nods. "I took a singles cruise there and did the tourist version." She blushes a little at the word "singles."

I glance at her hand. No ring. I picture swimming through blue-lighted water with her and find that it has a definite appeal.

"So it's for tourists?" I ask. That definitely makes it less interesting.

"There are tours and then there are *tours*," she says. "The locals can take you on private expeditions that wouldn't be appropriate for people who aren't comfortable taking some risks in the ocean."

Now that is starting to sound better. "Okay, I'm listening."

She smiles again. "I can forward you some ideas," she says. "How much time do you have?"

"I won't know when I need to report until my new assignment is made, but probably a month."

She nods. "Okay, then the cruise will work. It's just ten days. You'd be back in time."

"What's in it for my father?"

She shrugs. "I think he hopes you'll be so enamored with travel and leisure you won't go back to the SEALs." She downs the rest of her drink. "But I can see it's in your blood. You'll go back."

She slides out of her seat. "I'll send you the information." She stands and tugs out her phone. "Email or text?"

"Hey!" I say, standing next to her. "What's the hurry?"

Now she tilts her head, and her lashes come up slowly. I figure this look is something she uses on a lot of guys, but damn, it still works.

"It seems like we've made a deal," she says. "I know when to walk away."

Hell. I don't want her to go. Farther down the bar, a bass guitar cranks into gear. "Sounds like there's a live band starting," I say quickly. "We should check them out."

Vivienne pauses, as if weighing her decision. She looks over at the stage, then back at the door. Then at me.

I hold out my hands. "I'll buy you another drink. Just one."

"Okay," she says. "Just a drink."

I catch up with the waitress as we walk over and give her my room number for the bill.

Then we head to the bar, this devilishly sexy woman, and me, hot on her tail.

16: Vivienne

Holy hell I cannot keep up this classy act much longer.

This guy is literally the most ripped, bulked-up sex God I have ever laid eyes on. Even in a hoodie and jeans, he's like a supercharger, all shoulders and giant arms and broad as a wall.

I've played it light and easy, but the whole time we discussed kitesurfing and glowing ocean water, I was picturing body shots off his abs. This is one guy who could do that thing I always see in movies where the girl rides him while he's standing up.

It looks like a helluva workout for the man.

And yes, I want to do it.

I've finally met the man.

The dress swishes against my knees as we walk

toward the band. It's harder rock and roll than I generally like, but live music is live music. The bass guitar thumps in my belly, and each strum of the melody makes me want to break out in song.

Of course, I have no idea what they're singing. I could never understand the words in all the crashing cymbals and guitar licks. But I always appreciate a musician. I'll love it no matter what they do.

John and I settle at a little table near the back. There's a smattering of people in there, but as the band launches into a new number, they play like it's Radio City Music Hall.

"They're good," John says, leaning in close to talk in my ear.

"And loud!" I say.

I get my first whiff of him, clean and fresh-scrubbed. Nothing fancy. Probably a guy like him just grabs the hotel shampoo and calls it a day.

The waitress comes and he orders a beer. I get one too. He doesn't seem to care what kind it is, just accepts her recommendation.

We listen to the band for a couple numbers. I sip my beer and notice he's not drinking much of his. Not a big boozer, I can tell. He ordered it for show.

The band takes a break. I realize John is pretty close, his knee next to mine. I think for a moment about the billionaire. Is he going to call me when he gets back from Hong Kong, when our clocks align again? Technically, he could have left a message for me to get in the morning.

But he didn't.

Time to face facts. He's done.

I have to move on to seventy-four. There's a candidate right beside me.

I've never seen anyone like him. The bull rider was pretty cut. And a few here and there were pretty fit.

But this Navy SEAL is a whole different order of magnitude.

I reeeeeally want to check it out.

Run my fingers along those abs. Circle both hands around those biceps.

To hell with it.

I'm going full Vivienne.

I turn to him, making sure one of my boobs connects with his arm.

He notices, and his eyes dip to my cleavage. Yep, right where I want him to go.

"You have a room here?" I ask.

Now his expression changes. His eyebrows go up. "You want to go up?" he asks. He frowns.

Hmm. That wasn't the reaction I was looking for.

The shame wave threatens to toss me onto rocks. He's into fit and skinny chicks. I get it. I don't qualify.

I shrug like I don't care. "Not necessarily." I turn my attention to the empty stage.

A girl comes out with an acoustic guitar. She drags a stool over to one of the mics and sits down. "Testing," she says in the mic and leans away when a whine of feedback floods the room.

Everyone winces, a few covering their ears.

She waits a moment for it to fade.

"Okay," she says. "Now you're all awake."

The room titters.

I focus in on her. Maybe cut and bronzed isn't my guy for tonight. It's fine. I think he's going to book the cruise. I'll be happy with the money.

Politeness for a fellow singer won't let me get up and leave while she's talking or singing. I'll wait out one song, then go.

"I'm filling in the break," she says. "I might not be quite as loud as you're used to. She flashes a look at the retreating band members, who throw up their hands.

Another titter. A few more people have filtered in. The room is maybe a third full. I'd be sweating bullets if I were her. It's hard to be up there with a bunch of empty tables between you and the audience.

They can just keep talking and ignore you. That sort of stuff rips my heart out.

"I wrote this song," she says. "It's pretty simple, but most people like it. It's called, 'I Shine.'"

She's forgotten to introduce herself. She must be nervous. I'm intent on her, no longer worried about Mr. Hot Abs by my side. I really want to hear her sing. She has a soulful look, sort of Janis Joplin, with long, wild brown hair and a black tunic shirt over jeans.

She strums a few chords, and when the first words come out, I'm struck dumb. She sings with a heavy, dark voice full of blues. I can feel her words in my soul. My eyes smart with tears right off.

From the depths of desperation
I climbed the walls of fear
Rose up to my salvation
Before my world could disappear

This girl. I feel a million things at once. Admiration. Shock. Jealousy. Yeah, that's there too. She's so good. I don't want the other band to come back. I just want to hear her all night.

John sits slung back in his chair, a leg kicked out. I can see him from the corner of my eye. I wonder if it's just me affected by her and turn to take a quick look. He likes her, I can tell. His chin is moving up and down just a bit.

But it's not like me. I'm mesmerized. I glance around at the rest of the room. It's a mixed bag, some watching and listening, others fooling around with food or drinks or the check.

The song goes on and I feel every word.

You said my sun had set
And I believed it when you left
But now I rise and every day
I shine.
I shine.
Without you.
I still shine.

I tear slips down my cheek and I quickly wipe it away. I'd never been in love like the way she says, but if it's worse than I feel after some of these one-nighters, God. How does anyone survive it?

I'm startled when John slips a hand in mine and squeezes. He's noticed I'm affected. Well, all right. At least I don't have to leave in a snit.

The girl finishes the song and the audience claps. I feel like we should be standing, screaming, weeping. But I pull my hand from John's and keep my admiration to robust applause.

I forget all about wanting to leave.

The girl looks around and seems to feel maybe she should take it up a notch. She starts strumming a lot faster. "You all should know the next one. I'd appreciate it if you sang along."

I want to stand up and shout, "Who are you?" She might have some stuff for sale, or up on YouTube. I could listen to her every day of the week.

But I sit tight, elbows on the table, waiting for what she's going to do next.

When she sings the opening line, I lose it. I'm up, I'm cheering, and nobody's going to make me sit this one out.

It's "Girl on Fire."

This is my life theme song. And I can kill it like anybody.

She smiles my direction as she hits the first "ohhhhohhohoh" section.

I glance over at John, completely forgetting anything I might have been mad about before. There is nothing like live music with talent. That's why I love karaoke. It cuts from one singer to the next quickly. You suffer through the bad ones to get to those rare golden voices, the perfect pairing of singing and song.

To John's credit, he stands with me, clapping

along, swaying with me. A lot of people are sitting nonchalantly at their tables, and this pisses me off big time. I start moving, motioning people up.

As they start to rise, the girl says, "Sing it with me," and I'm on it, sidling up to old men and moms and teens and getting them in on the "ohhhohohoh" part.

John stays at his table, and honestly, I couldn't care less what he thinks. If he wants to slink out in embarrassment, don't let the door hit him in his ass on the way out.

We've got a pretty good crowd going now, and the girl wisely circles back around to add an extra chorus. I'm singing at the top of my lungs, encouraging more to join in. Several people motion me to go up on stage.

No way. This is that girl's spotlight.

But they get more aggressive, and when I look up, the girl herself is urging me to come.

Well, I'm not one to ignore an invitation like that.

I wind through the last tables and take the two quick steps up to the platform. She strums a little faster and shifts aside so I can join her at the mic.

We run through the last "girl on fire" and the room goes kind of wild.

I wrap my arm around her. "What's your name?"

I ask her into the mic.

She pinks up a little at this, probably finally realizing she never introduced herself. "I'm Adrianna Martinez and this is…"

Oh, crap. Really? I lean in. "Vivienne Carter."

The crowd starts chanting something and I look at her to see if she understands what they are saying.

"Duet?" she asks into the mic, and everyone shouts.

The audience is moving up close now. This is sort of crazy. I look out, since the lights aren't too blinding on this tiny stage, and see John pushing everyone forward.

Okay, maybe he's all right.

Adrianna steps back a few steps to avoid having the mic pick her up. "What do you know?" she asks.

"Everything!" I say.

"Upbeat or slow?" she asks.

I look out. "They're pretty riled. I say keep it fast."

"I only have time for one more," she says. "I'm just the break."

I nod. "How about something they will all know?"

"Everything I can think of is slow!" she says.

"*Grease*," I say. "You're the One That I Want."

She laughs. "Why not?" She picks out a few notes on her guitar. "That key going to work?"

"I'll wing it," I say. "Who's Danny and who's Sandy?"

"I'll take Danny first and you take him second."

I nod. "Let's do it."

When she picks out the opening melody, everyone cheers. It tends to be a crowd pleaser. The older crowd remembers the original movie. The young ones saw the live version on TV.

I've known the lyrics since I was ten. Mom loved it. I never told her she was singing the wrong words to "Greased Lightning." She might not have liked it so much if she had to change "scream" to "cream."

Adrianna belts out her first line, and just like we'd hoped, the dudes in the crowd are all over it.

I lead the ladies, and the song is off and running.

I have never laughed so hard on stage. Or had so much fun. And that's with three years of Mondays at FreakEasy. I'll have to find someone to do this with me there. For whatever reason, nobody brings this one up. That's about to change.

When the song comes to its final "oo oo oo," we all throw up our hands for a cheer. I think half the hotel might be in this part of the bar, as it's twenty deep from the stage.

I look out, trying to spot John, but it's a sea of faces in the semi-dark.

The original band comes out and thanks Adrianna for warming up the crowd for them. They've conveniently forgotten they already played a whole set.

I think it's bunk that they're going to take over when Adrianna got everyone going, but she nods politely at them and heads off stage.

I follow her down.

"You were so great," I say. "I'm at FreakEasy every Monday if you ever want to rotate in. Tell Mariah I sent you."

"Vivienne, right?" she asks.

"Yeah."

"It was fun."

She takes off through the crowd, who are already sitting down again as the band starts its first number. It's a real gift, being able to read a crowd and direct their mood. These guys are energetic and good, but they don't have that magic yet.

I wind my way back to my table. I've left my purse there.

John has returned to it and stands behind my chair.

"You were amazing," he says.

I pick up my bag and shoulder it. "Thanks."

I hesitate a moment, looking over his incredible frame, that killer jaw. This one isn't working out. My high from singing is wearing off, and I see things as they are. He's in town for a short while. If I go for this, it's just another temporary fling in a long line of them.

I should take a break from the one-offs for a bit. It's killing me.

"We could go upstairs now if you like." He gestures for the door.

I hesitate. But I remember his reaction from earlier, his eyebrows raised, the "You want to go up?" like he's shocked that I'm so easy or not in his league or whatever.

"I'm going to call it a night," I say. "You've got my info. If you want to do some travel, a little daredevil action, let me know."

And with that, Vivienne Carter *struts* to the door.

Alone.

Away from the hottie.

Into the January night.

Man. I'm going to hate myself in the morning.

17: Vivienne

Two more days go by. No word from military John.

I wish I hadn't spent most of that half-commission on an outfit since it looks like I won't be getting any more. The cruise is in two weeks, and honestly, bull rider and billionaire better get their money to me or they aren't going either. It's booking up.

All my bonus cash is going up in smoke.

Sam takes me to lunch on Thursday to try and bust my misery ball right open so the pus can drain out.

"You got to move on," she says. "Get right out there and have a good time again."

Easy for her to say. She didn't get her hopes up

on men *and* money.

All this is to say I'm a little surprised when we get back to the office and Janet flags me down. "Some young man left a message," she says. "He needs you to call his cell the minute you can. I tried to help him, but I don't know anything about cliff diving."

My heart skips a beat. It can't be a coincidence. I glance down at her note. Sure enough. John Jacoby.

I sit at my desk and dial the number as quickly as I can. Did somebody stiff him on a reservation? Or worse, is he hurt? I picture that pretty face bleeding and feel a little faint.

He picks up on the first ring. "Vivienne?"

"That's me," I say.

"Cliff diving. I loved it," he says. "I want to do more. Did you say there was cliff diving on this cruise thing dear old Dad wants to pay for?"

"Sure," I say, turning to my computer to look up the full itinerary. "Plus the kitesurfing."

"Yeah, I want to do that too. When's it leave again?"

"Eleven days from now," I tell him.

"Put me on it."

He's breathing hard and I can hear the excitement in his voice. He's flying high.

"I want to know everywhere I can cliff dive in

Florida in the meantime. Can you book them for me?"

"Sure," I say. "Give me a couple hours. How much you want to do?"

"Every day," he says. "Every damn day."

"Okay." I jot down some notes. "Give me an email so I can send you an itinerary and costs and all that."

"Send the bill to my dad. Tell him that's the price for going on his little excursion and putting up with his cronies." He hesitates. "He's not going to be on there, is he?"

"I can't see the full list, but he would probably have booked through me. I can find out discreetly when I talk to him," I say. "Is that a deal breaker?"

"Hell, yes," he says. "I'm about to jump here again. Call me this evening."

"Okay."

"Wait, better yet, meet me at the hotel again. Tonight."

My tummy flutters. "Your hotel?"

Sam looks up from her desk.

"Yeah. If that's okay."

"Maybe." I resisted him once. Not sure I can do it again. Plus he's going on the cruise with Mitch and Brady. The odds are going up that somebody would meet.

"That girl is playing again tonight," he says. "The one you sang with."

Now I hesitate. That was fun.

"It was just three songs, though," I say.

"No, full set. The other band moved on. The hotel really likes her."

"You been going down to hear her?" Maybe he's hooking up with her. A tendril of jealousy unfurls.

"I listened in last night. She did the *Grease* thing again. Wasn't the same without you, though. I forget her name. She forgot to introduce herself again. She needs you!"

Okay, now he's convincing me.

"All right," I say. "As long as I can get things booked by then." I glance at the clock. Damn, already after two. "Let me call your father."

"Excellent. See you there. Around seven?"

"Okay."

I hang up the call, and Sam is on me like a bee to a hive.

"Who was that? What are you doing?"

"It was the military guy. And I have shit-ton of work to do now." I twist my hair up on top of my head and stick a pencil through it. That's how you know it's gotten serious.

"Let me help," Sam says.

I set her looking up cliff dives. I'm happy to hand those commissions to her.

Then I call the dad.

I get his voice mail but tell him the cruise is a go and that John would like to prepare for some of the port activities here in Miami. I forward him the additional costs plus payment information and ask him to let me know if he will also be going on the cruise, as cabins are becoming limited.

Sam and I work on the cliff diving all afternoon, and I get a head start on the extreme sports package for all the port stops along the cruise itself. He's going to have a great time.

Dad's secretary calls back to let me know he approved the extra expenditures and will send in the deposit as soon as he gets confirmation from John that he's going. The extra commission will go to my account once the boat sets sail. She also let me know he'd be in Hong Kong all month, and that he would not be needing a spot on the cruise.

Her mention of Hong Kong makes me a little nostalgic for Mitch the Billionaire. I wonder if he's back yet. If he's thought of me.

Ugh.

Listen to me, mooning over the impossible.

Jerk.

He better delete those photos off his phone.

I comfort myself with thoughts of another evening with military boy as I package up the application and information to take with me tonight. I didn't take a picture of him the other day, so it's a good thing he suggested meeting again. I would've had to see him for that anyway.

I don't have another dress as fancy as the one I bought for the first meeting, but I'm not going to waste any more money until the big commissions start coming in. I did, however, send a note to Blue Sapphire Yachts that I had three pending bookings for the Cayman itinerary and to please hold cabins until I got the deposits.

Not that I'm for sure about Brady or the billionaire. It's been a week of silence at this point.

Maybe they're going to bail.

I park outside the hotel. I have on a big gray puffy coat because the temperature has gotten stupidly cold for Miami. I did not sign up for anything below fifty degrees when I moved here. The coat is from high school and I'm embarrassed to even be wearing it.

Mother Nature has GOT to be in menopause. She has cranked up the AC like my mama used to do.

I can't bear to wear the coat into that fancy place, so I ditch it in the car and run on high heels for the entrance.

The current of warm air when I enter the foyer is like heaven. Or, hell, I guess, since it's a hot blast in my face. I pause by a mirror and make sure my hair isn't a disaster and head to the bar.

The location where John is seated will tell me a lot about him. If he's any old place, then he's not a sentimental type. But if he's asked for the same booth as Tuesday, then maybe he's thinking fondly of me, or at least wants to make it easy for me to find him. I'll take either. Fondness or courtesy.

My feet go slow, giving my eyes time to adjust to the dim room. The bar is empty, and the few people around are scattered.

I don't spot him at any of the tables, so I head to the row of booths. We were in the second one.

And he's there.

Awww.

I like him again.

He's eating a big plate of barbecue. Like a platter of it. I guess defying physics makes you hungry.

"How was the second cliff dive?" I ask as I slide opposite him in the booth.

He swallows. He's a little more dressed up today

in a button-down shirt. I spot the chain of his dog tags before it disappears below the collar. The vision of him shirtless and seeing those metal tags starts to take seed.

"Less amazing," he says. "I need new spots. Higher jumps. Deeper water. Fewer tourists." His words are like a fountain bubbling over as he goes on about the rush of falling, the annoying people who chicken out and take forever to jump or bail. The importance of landing right, so the water doesn't break you in two.

He's killing me. I'd belly flop my way right into the afterlife.

"Wasn't it cold?" I ask. "It seriously dropped in temperature today."

"Nah. That didn't happen until late in the day. And I'm used to extremes."

"I bet."

"Brandy again?" he finally asks, realizing he's rambled.

I shake my head. "I'll stick to beer."

"Did you have dinner?"

"I'm good," I say. Sometimes I have zero trouble eating in front of a date, but right now I'm more self-conscious than usual. It's all the talk of healthy pursuits, exercise, climbing cliffs just to jump off. And imagining skinny girls in bikinis, and his absolutely cut body. I'm like a big blob of couch potato compared to all that.

Maybe all this was a bad idea.

We're like Mutt and Jeff.

Curse that shame wave. *Back off.*

We decide to wait on drinks until we've moved to the stage. John scarfs his meat. That boy can put it away. I think of Mitch and his seed salad. Takes all kinds.

I show him the application. I try to take a picture of him, but it's way too dark. I tell him I'll try again later, in the lobby maybe, and we head to the other room for more live music.

I'm excited.

18: John the SEAL

Vivienne is really something.

The singer is setting up when we walk into the stage area. I can sense Vivienne's excitement as we take a table right up front this time.

We order our beers, and Vivienne waves at the girl. She seems super stoked to see Vivienne again and steps down. The two whisper together, coming up with some ideas for numbers. Looks like Vivienne will be up there again.

This is fun. I've known a lot of women and had quite a number of short-term flings. It's not easy to get into anything serious when you're a SEAL. I spend huge chunks of time on boats or in locations where there can't be anyone but military personnel. It's just not possible. Even if I do ask for six months on land, it doesn't seem fair to start something when I'll just be gone again.

But Vivienne has that extra spark you don't see too often. She loves life and it shows.

I'm just not sure how far to take this. She was interested Tuesday, but I blew that with my surprised reaction. She's being far more standoffish today, talking business. She's way more into this singer than me.

"Don't forget to introduce yourself!" Vivienne shout-whispers as the girl heads back up.

She nods with a laugh. Her guitar strap goes over her head as she settles on the stool.

"Hello," she says in the mic. "I'm Adrianna Martinez, and welcome. I'm going to sing a couple originals, and then we'll get into the audience participation portion of the evening." She laughs. "Don't worry. Drink a little more and you'll be all good."

Vivienne lets out a whoop and a few others join her. I know she'll work the room for Adrianna if need be. And already, her enthusiasm is loosening up the people around us. I spot a few who were there the other nights. A fan club is growing. It'll get easier as more repeats start showing up.

This girl is savvy. Maybe it comes naturally to her.

Maybe her zest for life is catching.

Adrianna sings her "I Shine" song first, then a song about her daddy's race car. Both are good.

Then she waves Vivienne up on stage. Adrianna strums for a bit and announces they'll be singing, "Don't Go Breaking My Heart."

Now that is on point.

I sit back, arms crossed, and wait for them to start.

But I shouldn't have worried it would be some missile directed at me. They glam it up, singing to each other, then walking around and singing to random members of the audience. There's lots of laughs as Vivienne sits on some elderly man's knee and puts on his ball cap for a verse.

He doesn't want to let her go, and I stand up and act tough, lifting my fists like a Scrappy Doo "lemme at him" parody. This gets more laughs, especially when the old man stands and sings, "Don't go breaking my jaw."

Vivienne laughs so hard that Adrianna has to sing without her for a few notes. The whole audience is having a great time. I feel so proud of them both, even though I have nothing to do with it. I'm just pleased to have the association.

They do the *Grease* number, and everyone's

singing. They manage to get the boys on the opposite side of the room as the girls, and the bar becomes a madhouse.

By the time Adrianna finishes out the set and Vivienne sits back down by me, you'd think the place was a rave or something. Everyone's drinking and singing and happy.

"You know how to light up a room," I tell her.

"I do a lot of karaoke," she says. "It's a skill you pick up."

"Well, you are amazing at it."

"Thanks."

She takes a drink of her beer and frowns. "Warm beer," she says. "I might rather drink monkey piss."

God, she makes me laugh. "Shall I get you a fresh one?"

She shrugs. "I should probably go. We need to get your picture."

I don't really want to see the evening end, so I take a risk. "I think the lighting is good in my room."

She looks at me hard in the face. "Didn't that ship sail two nights ago?"

Damn. Okay. I'll take my lumps. But maybe I can turn this around.

"I just didn't think for a second someone as amazing as you would be interested in a dumb lug like me."

It's not a total line. My friends all got their degrees and went into SEAL training as officer candidates. I dropped out of school after two years. Sitting in a classroom writing essays was not my thing. I enlisted instead.

It's something I'm reminded of every day. My dad thinks I can redeem myself by going into politics now. My military service will count for something there.

"I don't think you're a dumb lug," she says. "And I'll personally scratch out the eyes of anyone who says so."

"Come on," I say. "Let's go up."

She looks me in the face one more time, hesitating. A couple people in the crowd come up and shake our hands, thanking Vivienne for a good time.

This helps her, I think. She's riding a high.

"All right," she says when we're alone again. "For the picture and maybe a drink."

I gather the paperwork and we head to the elevators. When I press the button, she says, "Did you know some buildings have private elevators just for the rich people?"

I laugh. "I guess they don't want to mix with the peasants."

"I wonder if there's one here." She glances around the lobby.

"Probably well hidden or with its own back entrance," I say. "I saw a few of them growing up. My dad's a senator. We often used back entrances for security reasons."

The doors open and we step on.

"I can see that. Your father is very…insistent," she says. "Apparently he's in Hong Kong. So no threat to your cruise."

"Yeah, but there's some guy on it he wants me to meet. That's going to be lame."

"Make him cliff dive with you. That should show your absolute supremacy." She smiles at me with that head tilt of hers. Dang, she's a knockout, eyes still all sparkly from the singing.

I want her to sing just for me.

My eyes rake her body as the elevator rises. She wears a siren red dress with a squared off neckline. She has a rack that won't quit. I'm picturing it already, all of it. I'm dying to know the color of her nipples.

She looks everywhere but me — the panel of floor numbers, the ceiling. I can't imagine she's a shy one. Or a wilting virgin. She knows how to work a situation. I'll definitely hand her that.

I'm feeling the months it has been since I last

held a naked woman in my arms and find I need this one more than I initially thought. Asking her here tonight was just an impulse, but now I realize my dick was thinking ahead of my brain.

The door opens, and each step down the hall feels like a mile. She's still acting all evasive, swishing her skirt and looking at the decor. Anywhere but me.

I decide to take charge of the situation and grasp her hand. I step away and whirl her in a circle, then pull her close. She lets out a little whoop.

Then we're dancing down the hall, a fast quickstep. She knows how it goes and follows my lead. I whirl her again, loving how her skirt spins out. I get a nice look at her bare legs before I pull her close and we finish out the distance to my room.

"What was that?" she asks as I shove the key card in the slot.

"I just wanted to dance with you."

"Huh," she says. "You didn't strike me as the dancing type."

I lean close to her ear and say, "I'm full of surprises."

She shivers a little, and I know that's a good sign. We're back on track.

I open the door.

"Now that's a room," she breathes.

"Yeah, Dad likes to remind me how I ought to be living." I toss the card on the counter of the wet bar. "Workout room sucks though."

She walks through the living space, her fingers trailing along the gold sofa. There's a fireplace and French doors to a balcony.

"It's beautiful," she says.

"It suits you," I tell her.

She turns and tosses me a look that says, "Cut the flattery." But I mean it. Maybe she doesn't recognize how glorious she is.

I'm going to be more than happy to show her.

19: Vivienne

Well, this is certainly a turnaround.

I don't know, maybe I screwed up my reaction to *his* reaction two nights ago. But John's all over me today, that's for sure.

I had no idea he could dance. Doesn't fit my image of a Navy SEAL, falling backwards off of rubber rafts.

I like him.

I like how his face gets all animated and his hands go wild when he talks about cliff diving. He really is an adrenaline junkie.

Which makes me wonder how he likes things in bed. I bet he is wild as hell.

God, I'm doomed. I'm totally going to sleep with this guy.

The room is delish. Earth tones and gold. A fireplace. A wet bar.

John digs around in the fridge. "Beer or liquor?" he asks.

"Is there some rum in there?" I ask.

"Yup." He plops a mini bottle on the counter. "With coke or straight up?"

"Diet coke."

He pops up. "The chemicals in that stuff will kill you."

"So will diabetes."

"You got diabetes?"

"No, but…" I trail off. I don't need to go into all this. "It doesn't matter. I'll take it either way."

He's a health nut. I figured. I probably could use the good example.

My gramma has diabetes. And I don't want it.

"Just don't get fat," my mama kept telling me, her eyes dropping to my hips.

I'm *fine*, Mama, now get out of my head while I sit in this hotel with a good-looking SEAL.

John mixes the rum and coke and pours a soda for himself, virgin-style.

"You don't like to drink, do you?" I slide up onto one of the stools by the bar.

"Not my thing. Makes you lose your edge."

"Yeah, hangovers would be a beast for half the stuff you do."

"That's how people die," he says. He hands me a glass, then clinks it with mine.

We both take a sip, eyes meeting.

"My coworker Sam and I planned all your stops on the cruise," I say. "I sent the bill to Dad."

"Nice, thank you."

"And Sam really went all out finding more cliff diving spots for you. I figured you'd be willing to drive to other cities. If not, we can cancel some."

"No, that's perfect."

We fall quiet. The ice maker under the bar drops a load, a tinkling crash in the silence.

John comes around and sits on the stool next to me. Our knees brush against each other. "How long have you been singing?" he asks.

"Since I could follow a tune," I say.

"You say you do karaoke. You ever try to make a demo?"

"I've made three," I say. I fool with my skirt, acting like I need to smooth it down. Navigating conversations about my failed auditions is always hard.

"I sure would like to hear one of those."

"I'm much better in person."

"Well, I can definitely attest to that."

I give him a small smile. "Do you sing?"

"Only if I want to scare off the local wildlife," he says.

Now that's funny. "I can't imagine not feeling confident in my voice," I say.

"It's a gift. One I definitely do not have."

"I don't believe you. Sing me something."

John props his elbow on the counter and drops his chin in his hand. "Trust me when I say, you most certainly do not need that pain in your life."

"Try me."

He pauses a moment, waiting to see if I'll let it go.

Not going to happen. I watch him while I drink. And drink.

"Okay, okay," he says. "But don't say I didn't warn you."

I like that he's willing to try.

He thinks for a moment. "I guess I'll make it simple," he says.

Then he starts singing.

Take me out to the ballgame
Take me out with the crowd

He stops at that moment.

I'm holding in everything. Because he was right.

It's bad.

So bad.

"I love it," I say, lying like a bearskin rug. "Keep going."

Buy me some peanuts and cracker jack
I don't care if I never get back.

At this point I join in. I've figured out how he gets off tune and know how to turn it around.

Let me root root root for the home team
If they don't win it's a shame

His eyes widen as he realizes what I'm doing. I'm able to harmonize with his off notes, which makes the song strange and wonderful. Not exactly the song as it was meant to be, but something entirely new.

For it's one, two, three strikes you're out
At the old ball game!

"How did you *do* that?" he asks, reaching out to grasp both of my hands.

"Years of duets," I say. "And a lot of church choir harmonies with warbly octogenarians."

"You made me sound good!" His eyes are on fire, alight with the fun of having succeeded.

He stands up and pulls me off the stool. "Do it again!"

And so we sing it again, this time dancing around the sofa.

At the end, he whirls me around, lifting my feet off the ground. "You are literally the most fun I've had in six years."

"What happened six years ago?" I ask.

"I enlisted."

"You don't like it?"

"No, I love it. But we do serious work. I mean, we cut up. And the men in my platoon…I'd give my left nut for them." He sets me down and holds my hand high, turning me in circles around him, like I'm in his orbit. "But this is different."

He stops me and pulls me close to him. "You are unbelievable."

His eyes hold mine, and my breath catches. I'm a total sucker for this feeling. Completely. It's like my oxygen.

He leans closer, and my lids close as his mouth meets mine.

His lips play with me, tempting and warm. His body is rock hard against me. I've never felt a chest like his. I move my arms between us to feel the sharp delineation of each muscle.

A fire starts to lick through me. An opportunity like this doesn't come along often. I should take it.

His hands start to drift along my body, hips then waist, his thumb flirting with the side of my breast.

I'm on board, totally, and as his cock starts to take up more space between us, I'm ready to see all of this boy.He reaches down for the hem of my dress and lifts it, baring my legs. Then his hands slide behind my thighs, lifting me up.

God, he's doing the thing where he stands while I straddle him! I lock my ankles behind him, and his body thrusts against me, the jeans sliding along my inner thighs.

Now I'm on fire. I want to do this. It's my biggest running fantasy. I cling to his neck, our tongues meeting. I can feel him between my legs. I want these clothes *gone*. I want him there.

Now now now now.

I break the kiss. "Can we do this position naked?" I whisper in his ear.

His cock goes wild, straining against me. I'll take that as a yes.

He lets me down, yanking off his shirt and reaching for the snaps to his jeans. I've never seen anyone undress as fast as he is right now.

I lean against the back of the sofa, watching. My God, this is better than any strip club. He's cut everywhere, and my eyes don't know where to look. The eight-pack abs? The chiseled chest? Those outrageous biceps? I want to melt into a quivering pile.

The tight shorty boxers come down and yep, that's where I want to be looking. He springs out at me like a John-in-a-box. I'm zinging in all the good places.

And I want that *in* me. Stat.

"Your turn," he says.

I kick off the red heels. John towers over me now, which is nice, as it gives me a sense of feeling dainty as I fight any self-consciousness. He leans back against the counter of the bar, his cock straight out. I can't take my eyes off it.

The dress unzips in the back, and it's not the most graceful thing to reach it.

"Let me," he says and steps forward.

His engorged dick pokes against me as he gets close. I want to reach out and give it a long lingering stroke, but it disappears as John moves behind me to unzip the dress.

Cool air hits my skin as it gets exposed. Then his lips press into the back of my neck.

I'm on fire. He pushes the dress off my shoulders until it puddles on the floor.

His hands are everywhere, belly, breasts, hips. I feel my bra loosen, then it lands on the dress.

And the panties slip down.

He's still behind me, warm and muscled.

"Let's see where you are," he says. His hand slides down my back and between my legs.

I suck in a breath as a finger slips inside my body.

"So wet," he says. He walks us closer to the sofa and presses me forward so I bend over it.

More fingers go in, and I'm feeling lost, hands braced on the back of the sofa. It's very slippery down there. Just the sight of him got me way over the edge.

He finds the nub and starts working it. Jesus. I breathe deeply as the tension starts to build.

His free hand comes around to knead a breast, tweaking the nipple. I press back into his hand, feeling his cock against my thigh. I want that thing.

"Please," I say. "Just take me."

He withdraws his hand a moment and reaches for his jeans on the floor. I hear the telltale rattle of a condom wrapper. Then he's back, hand around front, his cock sliding into place.

"How hard do you like it?"

"However an adrenaline lover like you can dish it out."

He pauses. "You mean it?"

A thrill zips through me. "You have an idea?"

"I do."

He stands me up and takes my hand, leading me to the balcony.

Oh, shit. What have I done?

The door slides open, and the chill sends goosebumps across my skin.

"You game?" he says.

"You going to keep me warm?" I ask.

"I do so solemnly swear."

I nod.

He turns me to him and drags my body against his. He's hot and hard. His hands go to my waist to lift me up, and I wrap my arms around his neck.

He fits himself against me, then slams my hips down, entering me with a wild thrust.

"Shit!" I say. "God!"

We stand by the open door, the cold washing over my back, but heat building in my arms and legs. He lifts me up and slams me down, over and over, each time creating a shock wave that blasts up my body.

I want to cry out, to scream. I'm dizzy and high, elated and losing track of which way is up or down.

He steps out onto the balcony, but I don't feel the cold now at all. This position is work, not just for him, but for me. The exertion makes the pleasure more extreme.

Probably people can see us, but I don't even care. I want them to see. Look at this cut god holding me up, slamming me onto his cock. I want video. I want prime time. Pay a subscription fee, suckers, because this is gold.

He holds me still and rotates inside me, grinding against every sensitive part.

I lose it then, and the orgasm starts in a ring around where we join, then explodes out like a grenade going off.

I'm crying out, and crying for real, exhausted and exhilarated and on the edge of really truly dying.

We move again, and I realize he's climbed a chair and we're on the pillar that holds the rail to the wall. Shit, we're practically on a ledge, and he pushes me against the wall.

The danger makes it so intense that the orgasm never really stops. It builds right back in. I don't care about falling, or dying, just living. Right here, with this man holding on to me, shoving his cock straight into my soul.

He loses it then, pulsing into me with a tribal cry. Tiny bits of shocking cold bite into my skin and I think I've gone over some threshold. Only as he holds on to me, pressing me into the wall do I realize it's rain. We're outside on a ledge, ten stories, up, naked, his cock inside me. And it's raining.

Holy shit.

"You okay?" he whispers in my ear.

I nod. I'm more than okay. I'm a damn goddess. I cheat death. I screw on ledges!

I'm high as a heroin addict as he carefully pulls out of me and helps me step down onto the chair. Then he leaps down.

We dash back inside, wet and shivering.

"We made it rain!" he says, laughing and drawing me against his body again.

"Was that us?" I ask, laughing too, giddy and flying on elation.

"It was!" He takes my hand and leads me to the bedroom and into the giant bathroom. He turns on the shower, and in only a moment, the whole room is full of hot steam.

"Come in," he says, opening the glass door and taking my hand.

I step gingerly into the spray. He's going to get raw me, no makeup, wet hair. The whole deal.

But the shame wave can't touch this crazy high I feel. We cling to each other in the spray, the world foggy and gray from steam. He kisses me and washes me and gets on his knees to press his mouth between my legs.

I hold on to the walls, water tumbling down my body. I'm lost in this man. Utterly, totally lost.

One more orgasm, then two when he bends me over the tile shelf, knocking all the hotel toiletries to the floor. We collapse into bed, exhausted and spent. I hurt in a hundred places and can't resent a single one.

And even when I wake up in the wee hours, four a.m. according to the clock, I don't leave.

I'm hooked.

20: Vivienne

OMG I am so late.

I don't often stay the whole night with a new man, and here I am in a hotel with blackout curtains, and I have slept like the dead.

Which I should be. Dead, that is. Good God Almighty, I had sex on a ledge! In the rain!

What seemed daring and wild last night seems really risky and stupid this morning.

I turn to John and realize he isn't there. What?

I sit up, dragging a sheet around me. My dress is in the other room. Oh, God, I'm a disaster. Rain, shower, insanity half the night. My hair is all over the place. I have nothing to fix it.

And I'm on the top floor of a fancy hotel.

This is going to be one epic walk o' shame.

As I cross the room, I hear water running. It's the shower. Okay, so John is in there.

I toy with going back in with him, but my screaming thighs say, uh, no. Dang it. I should work out more.

I laugh out loud. Who am I kidding? I consider gargling a form of exercise.

I hear a voice and pause by the bathroom door. It's mostly closed, but there's a crack. The room is steamy when I peek.

The voice is John.

Singing "Take Me Out to the Ballgame."

Too cute.

I sneak to the living room and pick up my dress and underwear. Unlike the night with bull rider, I'm getting fully dressed before I walk out of this place. I suddenly see the benefit of motels over hotels. Doors to the outside. A quick getaway. Here, I'll have halls and elevators and a big old lobby.

Sigh. I can do this.

By the time I have my clothes on, the water has gone off. I guess I can face this. Besides, I still need a picture of him.

Except.

Wait.

A memory comes back to me and I sort through

the evening. Sing. Ledge. Shower. Orgasm. Orgasm. Bed. Drinking. More sex. Pictures.

Pictures?

I search through my purse for my phone. Not there.

I head back to the bedroom.

Not on the side tables.

Not on the floor.

I rummage through the sheets.

Okay, there it is.

I glance at the bathroom door to make sure John's not coming as I power it up.

Dead. Figures.

I spot John's phone, nicely plugged into the wall. Fully charged.

I pull out the plug and stick it in mine. My face pinks up, imagining what all might be on there.

For long moments, the phone does nothing, gathering enough juice to turn on.

John hums to himself in the other room, off key, clearer now with the water off. A razor starts to buzz.

Come on, phone.

The screen lights up and I swiftly open the photos app.

Oh. My. Word.

The first image is to die for. John, naked, lying in

the sheets. I'm somewhere near his knees. His cock is huge, filling up a lot of the screen, and behind him, a blurrier chest and face. He's laughing.

I press the phone to my chest. Holy shit! He let me take that! I know he wasn't drunk.

And honestly, thinking back, I don't remember more than two drinks myself.

We were just high on each other. The crazy stuff we were doing.

It's hard to move past that one, but I swipe it aside. Next is a selfie of the two of us, cuddled together against the headboard. We're both naked, but he's taking the shot, so both my arms are wrapped around one of his, covering my boobs. It's not too bad, actually. My hair is slick and wet, but my mascara is sort of smoky smudged around my eyes, not dripping like an ugly cry.

There are more, but mostly blurry man chest and one extreme close-up of his butt. Then another keeper, him all twisted in the sheets, looking at me with bedroom eyes.

"Got some good ones?"

I nearly jump out of my skin.

John is in the doorway, looking close to perfect in sweatpants and nothing else. His chest and shoulders never fail to make me melt.

"Yes, but I still need one for the application." I try to sound all businesslike, but my voice is all husky. Dang, he's cut.

"Should I put on a shirt?" he asks.

Never. Not ever ever.

"Probably so," I say. "You need to look legit."

He laughs. "It might be fun to see how crazy I could look on the application so my dad has to force them to let me on."

He opens a closet door and pulls out a pale blue button-down. "But I guess there's no need to make more work for you." He slides it on, and I sorta want to pout. Goodbye, muscles.

"Just a head shot, right?" he asks, gesturing to the sweats.

"Yeah," I say. I let the phone charge a little more while I move him near the window until the light is good.

The phone gets up to five percent charged and I pull the cord. "Look right here," I say, and snap the shot. It's probably good to push that, ahem, *other* picture a little bit back in the list. Though I will probably be staring at it for nights to come.

"Look good?" he asks.

"Yeah," I say. Now comes the awkward part. The separation.

He steps up and plays with my hair. "You look freshly fucked," he says.

"Oh," I say. "Yes. I'm sure it's a mess."

"It's fine," he says. "Just wild. You have to work today?"

I nod. "And you have another cliff dive. One o'clock. It's supposed to warm up by then."

"Cool," he says.

We look at each other a moment, then he steps forward to pull me into his arms. "Did you book me every day or is there a time I can see you this weekend?"

Seconds with the wild man. I think I'm up for it.

"You have an opening on Saturday evening after six," I say. "Should I pencil me in?"

"You better."

He kisses me softly. I'd love to just sink back into him, but I'm scheduled to come in today. Janet holds me to the times I put down.

I pull away, holding his hand briefly before letting go. "Tomorrow, then?"

His smile devastates me. "Tomorrow."

I hurry to the living room for my bag. Now it is time to hustle.

But I'm seeing him again.

When I step into the elevator, I'm thankfully

alone.

So I can't help it.

I look to the ceiling.

And hollah, "WHOOP!"

21: Vivienne

When I get in the office, two hours after what I told Janet, Sam raises her eyebrows at me. "Some application meeting, eh?" she says.

"Yeah." I wave at Janet and shout, "Sorry!"

Janet shrugs. "You set the hours. Just try to abide by them."

She likes to bring in another travel agent if I'm taking time off. She's a fuddy duddy to talk to, but generally okay to work with. She doesn't make a fuss unless you're a walking disaster.

And since the office gets a cut off my commissions, she can't be too upset with my productivity. Three Blue Sapphire Yachts!

Except, what has happened to Brady and Mitch?

I get busy, putting in a call to Bonnie to ask if the

billionaire is still going on the cruise, as he hasn't confirmed. They are still in Hong Kong. Dang it.

Then I send an email to the bull rider asking the same thing. I let him know the cruise is booking up.

I type John's application into the system, and I feel good. Busy. Productive. A real working girl trying to make her way in the world.

Except, this isn't my dream. Making crummy commissions on other people's adventures. I glance over at Sam, then back at Janet. They are both occupied at the moment.

So I open up my tab of audition sites.

Mostly it's the same ol' bunk. Indie films wanting people to work for free. Scammers trying to get you to pay thousands to be discovered. Yada yada yawn.

Then something catches my eye. An invitation-only audition in Nashville with Gold Discography Records.

They're huge.

We have to send our social media links, number of followers, and our best YouTube video to try and score an audition with them.

I search around and see several forums have threads about it. It's legit, and everybody is scrambling to get their numbers up before they submit.

Dang. I glance up. Sam and Janet are still

occupied.

I head over to my YouTube channel. I have around eight hundred subscribers, which isn't horrible, but not major-label worthy.

What can I do? Mariah might let me pass something out at FreakEasy. I could probably get another fifty. I should at least be at a thousand before I sub.

I could cough up money to advertise one of my videos. But it's risky. For one, it's money I don't really have. And two, sometimes ads draw the trolls. Plus, if someone calls you out for paying to get subscribers, it's all over anyway.

Shoot.

I remember the bull rider said he had some fans. He offered to share my stuff.

I might have to take him up on that.

He needs to email me! I sit in front of the list of messages, willing a new one to pop up.

But nothing.

Shoot.

❊CℛℬↃ

I spend Saturday morning trying to decide what

to wear that evening with John. I'm not used to seeing someone for a third time. There's the wrap-around green dress I wore with Brady. And the ombré jewel dress I wore with Mitch.

I guess one of them will have to do since otherwise it's pants, which never fit me right, leggings, which seem too casual, or shorts, which definitely won't help since I'm pasty despite living in Florida. My legs are most certainly not my *best* asset. It is back up to eighty degrees, though. The cold front is long gone, and Miami is back to its proper spot on the thermometer.

I'm about to head to a resale clothing shop when my phone buzzes.

It's John. In a Facetime!

God, my hair! I look at myself on the screen and decide, actually, I'm looking good enough. I hit "accept."

"Hey!" I say, my heart suddenly sinking. Is he canceling tonight?

"Vivienne!" His hair is all spiky and he has on a wet suit of some kind. It's black and shiny.

"You cliff diving?" I ask.

"I just did one!" His voice has that elated quality I already recognize from an adrenaline high. "You busy?"

"No," I say, setting my car keys back on the coffee table. I glance to the open door of my roommate Carrie's room. She's nosy.

"I know cliff diving isn't your thing — yet," he says. "But I wanted to take you on this jump with me!"

What does he mean? I sure hope he's not asking me to leap off a perfectly good piece of ground.

But he sticks on a strange round hat with a little camera on the front.

"I'm borrowing a Go Pro with wireless. I'm going to send you a link on Periscope, so you can see what I see as I jump!"

My relief is so intense it's practically an orgasm. "Absolutely!"

"I'm texting you the link right now!" he says. He looks down as he punches on his phone.

"When are you jumping?" I ask.

He looks away at someone and gives a thumbs up. "Now! I have to end the call. But go to the link!"

He kills the connection and I scramble to find the text message and click on it. At first the video is all black, but then I see the sky, the ground, and then a super close-up of some guy.

"Let me make sure the waterproof housing is tight," the guy says. He has a mustache that curls on the ends. He fiddles with the camera and I mostly see his fingers for a minute.

Then he backs away.

"We online?" John asks. He must turn his head, because I see a flash of cliffs and ocean, then a close-up of several people. There's a guy on the back of a pickup truck, looking in a black plastic case.

He nods. "You are live."

"Hello, Vivienne!" he says, and puts his fingers in front of the camera for a little wave.

"Hello, John," I say back, even though I know he can't hear me.

He turns the other way, and I see a girl in a half-unzipped wet suit, showing off a skimpy red bikini top. When she sees he's turned to her, she cocks out her hip and tilts her head.

"Hey, John," she says. "Lookin' good."

I hate her.

Ugh.

I'd drive right down there except I helped research these places and he's a good hour away.

And he might ask me to jump.

No, thank you.

He looks away from the girl without even responding. This pleases me. A lot.

"You ready Jacoby?" someone shouts.

"Let's do it!" he says.

Someone shouts a word I can't make out. Then a small, distant shout comes from below.

My view is of the sky, the clouds, the ocean. It's breathtaking. I forget the scenery can be so amazing once you get outside the tight, overbuilt beaches of Miami.

Then the camera pans down. I'm seeing everything John does.

The water is below.

WAY down below.

There are huge jagged rocks on either side of him!

I'm totally panicked.

I cannot breathe.

He's HIGH! Too high!

Oh my God!

"Don't do it!" I scream, and Carrie and Emerald come rushing out of their rooms.

"What the hell?" Carrie yells.

I wave her away. John lines up his feet with a tiny corner of the rock.

Jesus. God. He's going to do it.

I can't even watch.

But I have to.

"What is this, some video?" Carrie asks, looking

over my shoulder.

"It's my boyfriend! This is live!" I shriek.

"You have a boy—" Carrie starts.

"Shush!" I command.

Okay, it's been two dates, but tonight will be three!

If he doesn't die.

People around him are obviously cheering. I can hear the muffled sound as well as the crash of waves down below.

I can't take it. I sink to the floor, holding the phone. Carrie and Emerald peer over my shoulders.

I'm not really close to those two. They're thick as thieves. I'm just there to help with rent. But they like to nose in on my life. I'm their favorite topic of gossip.

John's knees in the wetsuit appear. He bends.

"He's gonna do it," Emerald says.

I have to force my eyes open to watch.

Our view changes to open air.

"He's gone!" Carrie says.

"Look down!" Emerald shouts. "We want to see the water!"

We see his knees and feet sticking out. The world turns as he does a flip. Then he's straight up and down.

Then bubbles.

We're underwater.

For a moment the signal seems to cut out, frozen.

"Did he survive?" Carrie asks.

My heart isn't even beating. I'm dead.

He's smashed to bits somewhere.

Dead too.

Dead together.

Like Romeo and Juliet.

More bubbles appear, and the camera breaks the surface.

We hear cheers. His hands come up as he holds them overhead.

Then he's swimming, and I can see each arm as it comes forward.

"That dude is batshit crazy," Emerald says.

He's alive.

By God, he's alive.

I let out a breath.

"Huh, cool," Carrie says. "Where did you meet him?"

"The travel agency," I say. But my brain is still in shock. How can he do that stuff? It was terrifying just to watch.

The girls take off for their rooms again.

John reaches a shallow beach. A couple guys

there shake his hand.

"You see that Vivienne?" he asks.

"I did," I whisper.

The view goes wild and jagged, then I see John's face. He's taken off the helmet and turned it around. "See you tonight!"

Then the feed cuts out.

I can't get off the floor. I'm too freaked out.

This guy is like nothing I've ever seen.

He scares me. In a good way.

But still, he scares me.

22: Vivienne

Saturday night is like an ordinary date. We eat dinner. We walk along the beach.

No ledge sex. No jumping off cliffs. We're perfectly pedestrian, other than that naughty bit in a rocky spot along the shore around midnight.

I still have sand in random places from that.

Unfortunately, our cliff diving itinerary has him sleeping in other cities the next few nights.

So on Monday I'm back to reality and the travel agency.

Sam and I watch the video of his cliff dive together.

"That guy is Grade A loco," she says.

"He likes to live wild," I say.

"How are you going to have children with that?"

she says. "He'll want to go skydiving on your wedding day."

I click away from the link. "I doubt I'll have to worry about that. He doesn't live here."

"He could live anywhere," she says, sitting back. Her face has attitude written all over it. She wants me to have what I want. That's why I love her.

"He's going to re-enlist," I say.

This, I'm pretty certain of. I'm not sure we could even keep his adrenaline rush going with civilian adventures. He faces real life and death stuff in the Navy.

I don't show Sam *the picture*. Not any of them, actually. But I steal looks at the images as I work. He is something else. Like nothing I could have even imagined having for myself.

The shame wave has moved to a whole 'nother country.

Several messages come through from Sapphire. They still have three cabins open for me, but I need to get deposits in or they will let them go. The cruise is only a week away.

God. I call Bonnie again. Then leave a message for John's father. And email Brady. Why are all these people waiting until the last minute? I'm not a miracle worker.

I'm about to walk out the door at the end of the day when the notification that I got John's money comes through. Dang. I quickly forward it to Sapphire and try to set up his room.

A message comes up.

No deposit found for that guest.

There is too! I just sent it!

No deposit found for that guest.

How long does it take for it to go through?

I drum my fingers on the table. I can't access this system from home. I have to do it here.

No deposit found for that guest.

Gah.

An hour after everyone else has left, my stomach is growling like a bear and I only have thirty minutes until karaoke starts at FreakEasy. I need to make some little notices to pass out so people subscribe to my profile and get my numbers up for that audition with Golden Discography.

I have to kill it tonight to make sure everyone does it.

But I'm still at work!

I wait another ten minutes, then realize it's not going to go through tonight.

It must only get deposited during business hours. Manually. By snooty old ladies with bad attitudes.

Curses!

I'll book him first thing in the morning. If Sapphire has held the cabins like they said, it will be fine.

I scurry out the door to get home, doll myself up, type up my YouTube info, and get on the rotation.

And decide what to sing.

✿✧✿

FreakEasy is amazing as always. Mariah rotates me in four times. I do Shania. I do Dolly. The crowd goes wild for "You're the One that I Want," which I duet with one of the regulars.

I get home and check my subscribers. Twenty more.

Ugh. Not enough. I need two hundred!

I have to send in my info at the end of the day tomorrow.

I should write the bull rider. Tell him it's fine if he's bailing on the cruise. Will he forward my YouTube video?

I'll pick my most popular one. No, that's a cover. Record labels aren't impressed by singing someone else's song. They want to hear yours.

I spend hours clicking through my songs and

picking apart the mistakes, the outfits, the cluttered backgrounds, the dog that barked in the background.

I'm such an amateur.

I finally narrow it down to three with decent views and original songs. I'll pick one in the morning when I'm on my work computer and compose the email to Brady.

Sleep is fitful and short, and before I can really settle in, my alarm has gone off. I drag myself out of bed, thankful that my hair is sprayed so fantastically that the updo has more or less held up during my three hours of sleep.

Case in point number nine: I sometimes go to bed with toilet paper pinned to my 'do, just like my gramma.

This does *not* make me old fashioned.

But you knew that.

Despite my tiredness, I'm ready to work. I'm in my chair and typing before Sam has even said hello.

"Well, aren't you the busy beaver this morning," she says.

"One week until that cruise," I say. "I gotta get my money."

I know I should book John straightaway, but every hour counts if Brady's going to send out my link.

I write him quickly.

My bull rider,
It's totally cool if you decided against the cruise. I think it's overpriced anyway.

(And includes another guy I slept with.)

I had a great time with you. I will never look at that green dress the same way.

I want him to be picturing me when I say the next part.

You asked to see my YouTube videos, so I'm sending one. If you want to pass it along to some of your rodeo-loving fans, I'd be thrilled. A record label will be looking at this video soon, and the more love it has, the better my chances.

I paste in the link. And...send.

I let out a long breath. Sam looks up. "Break up with one of them?" she asks with a smile.

"Funny," I say, even though it's not. I haven't forgotten that both Brady and the Rich Mitch have totally gone silent.

But John makes up for it. Knowing our

relationship has an ending that we can't control is sort of nice. I just can't fall in love with him or anything. I have to take the wild ride and be ready to get off the horse.

I open my photo app and take another gander at that unbelievable X-rated photo. Jesus, Mary, and Joseph. What a man.

My email dings and I whip my chair around. Please be Brady!

But it's Bonnie. She's got Rich Mitch's deposit ready. *Yes!* She apologizes profusely for the delay. They had an unexpected trip to Hong Kong that became a week long. The time difference made it difficult to communicate with the office.

My belly flips. So Mitch is back.

The agency phone rings on line two. I glance back at Janet. She's on line one. I really don't want to get embroiled in a long conversation about who knows what. "You take this one," I tell Sam.

She picks up the line.

I quickly forward the money for Mitch to the cruise company. Thankfully John will be so busy with his adventure itinerary that he won't run into him. Probably Mitch doesn't even remember my name by now.

God, I hope they don't meet.

"Hey, Viv, it's for you," Sam says. She puts the call on hold. "Sounds like a billionaire!"

Oh, crap.

He doesn't need to call me. Bonnie already handled the trip.

Still, my heart hammers. I wanted him to call me for over a week.

But now there's John.

Except Mitch *does* live here.

Maybe after the cruise. After John is gone. Mitch is bound to be crazy busy before he has to take off again. No time for red sofa girls.

I take a deep breath and pick up the line. "This is Vivienne," I say.

"Now that's a voice I've missed," Mitch says.

Well, damn. My serial monogamy is in serious jeopardy.

"Hey," I say. "I heard you went to a very sinful city."

"Not near as sinful as it would have been if you were there."

This obviously isn't about business. And I don't know what to say.

My cell phone buzzes. It's John. He's thinking of me before he takes his next dive.

How did I get into this predicament?

"Did you have a good time?" I ask. Sam is watching me, not even hiding that she's listening to every word.

"Wretched, actually. What was supposed to be a simple meeting at my office a week ago became a long trip filled with tortured negotiations."

"They tortured you?"

"No, I tortured them. But I often do."

"Did you win?"

"More or less. Bonnie says you have the cruise all set up for me."

"I do."

"I don't guess I could interest you in going."

I almost drop the phone.

Holy shit.

My brain flashes in a thousand directions. A cruise. A one-hundred-thousand-dollar cruise. With the billionaire.

Except.

John is going.

God.

John.

I can't. I can't possibly.

My print-out for the record label competition catches my eye. The decision for that will be made in two weeks, which would be right in the middle of the cruise. I wouldn't be here to schedule my audition. Even if John wasn't on the boat, I couldn't go.

"I'm a working girl," I say. "Besides, I'm hopefully going to be booking a trip to Nashville. There's an audition, a big one with Gold Discography Records that I might get to do."

"Now that sounds promising." Mitch smoothly moves on to talking about the itinerary and asking about the ports. He's careful. He doesn't want to dwell on my turning him down or make me feel bad.

He's a gentleman.

He and John could not be more opposite.

I like both of them in different ways.

"My calendar is untenable until the boat sails," Mitch says. "But I hope I can see you when I return?"

Now, that I can do. John will be re-enlisting. I'll be alone again.

"I'd love that, Mitch," I say. "I really would."

"Good!" There's a note in his voice I haven't heard before. Upbeat. Optimistic. He wasn't sure if maybe I was making an excuse about the cruise. I'm pleased to have made him happy.

"See you soon," I say.

When I put the phone back on the base, Sam leaps up. "What! You going to see them both? Girl, you gettin' in over your head?"

"Nah," I say. "I won't see Mitch until after the cruise. John will be long gone by then."

"Unless your sweet nectar makes him give up the SEALs," Sam says.

I shake my head. "No, he loves it too much. And it's fine. It's not like I'm in love with any of them."

"True," Sam says. "That's one thing I've never seen. Vivienne in love."

It sounds so abysmal when she says it.

But it's true.

The type of man interested me tends to be obsessive and stalkerly. Crazy.

The type of man I tend to be interested in, well, they don't usually call me the morning after.

But now two have. John *and* Mitch.

I turn back to the Blue Sapphire web site. I have to book two cabins, and I don't want to keep talking about love, especially since both men are long shots for anything more than a fling.

My email dings, and holy crap, the bull rider has written me back! I scan the email quickly. He's sorry he's been delayed about the money. He had to drive to Nashville to track down a paycheck, and he's worried he isn't going to get the money together for the trip.

Bummer that it isn't working out. Poor Brady. He

pinned all his hopes on it.

I spot the word "YouTube" and quickly jump to it.

Yes, he says. He's going to send it out now.

Oh, yes!

I write back a very quick THANK YOU and hit send.

Now I have *got* to book these cabins.

I log into Blue Sapphire's system.

And…it's in use by another agent.

This is ridiculous. Why don't they update this thing? Why can only one agent book at a time?

But I can't scream at them, because there are only ten agencies approved, and it's big money. We're super lucky to be one. It wasn't Janet that got us in. She's just the manager. But the owner herself, Lucky Vega.

I know, she sounds like a porn star.

But she's a super-agent, concierge to the stars. She has an office in the back, but she's never here. She meets clients in person. I only met her once, a few months after Janet brought me on. She is one of those people who has *presence.*

And honestly, she's who inspired me to try vintage hair. She walked in looking like Greta Garbo and everyone stood at attention.

I switch over to my YouTube channel to see how the video is doing. I'm sure Brady hasn't done anything yet. He just wrote me. But there should be FreakEasy fans, and watching the count go up will give me something to do.

I have to send that sucker off tonight. Hopefully they won't look at it for a few more days, so it can gather more.

Every time I refresh, the ticker goes up two or three views.

It's something.

I go back in to Blue Sapphire, and it's still busy. Great.

I spend a couple hours going back and forth between my view count and the cruise site. Sam asks me to go to lunch, but I figure I should wait. Surely whoever is hogging the system will leave eventually.

"I'll bring you a sandwich," she says.

"You're the best," I tell her and click refresh on my video again.

Janet leaves too, so I end up taking a long call from a lady who wants to go to Paris on the cheap. So instead of refreshing YouTube, I look up flights and discount hotels and tours.

Sam comes back. "Still not in the system?"

I haven't checked in a while, lost in the rabbit

hole of Paris destinations.

I have two emails as well.

One is from Bull Rider. He's sent the video out and also taken out a little loan to cover the last of the cruise money. I should get it all from the bank any minute.

There's another email, but I have to go to YouTube first to see what's happened while I wasn't watching.

And yes, there's two hundred more views already! And almost one hundred more subscribers!

I go through all my videos, down another rabbit hole, hoping I chose the right one. For the next hour, my count continues to go up. Every time I try to break away to work, I'm dying to see what my count is now, and I'm sucked back in.

Then it happens.

I hit one thousand!

I did it!

I quickly write Brady another huge thank you.

And I see the bank message.

It's his money!

Wow!

I do a little jig in my chair. All three Blue Sapphire commissions are coming! Plus the triple for John.

I almost feel bad for taking that money.

But not bad enough to turn it down.

I forward the money to Blue Sapphire for Brady.

Then I head into the system to book the cabins.

And I'm in!

YES!

A text comes through, but I ignore it, scouring the cabin list to see where Blue Sapphire held my rooms.

And I don't see them.

What?

One of the cabins blinks blue, which means it is available to edit. Which is weird, as there is a name on it. Adolfo Felini.

But when I look, there are three with Adolfo Felini. Maybe these are the saved ones for me?

I get a text and an email at the same time, and my freak-out mode starts to fire up. There's too many demands on me at one time.

I take deep breaths, examining the cabins. Felini must be the Sapphire employee I talked to. That's why I can edit it. Hopefully when I change one, the others will come available.

I click on the blue one and start typing John's name.

A box pops up, "Add additional occupant?"

I've never had to do a booking like this before, so I'm not sure. I think I want to *replace* the occupant. When I say no, it kicks me out.

So I click again, type his name, and this time, say yes.

John Jacoby appears on the cabin line.

Okay, cool, it worked.

I get prompted, "Add another guest?"

I start to breathe easier. I'm not sure if Mitch's money has gone through yet. John's took all night.

Another text comes through.

I'll wait a minute. Give Mitch a little more time to process. Somebody else held up the system all day. I can have it for an hour.

Maybe they were waiting for deposits too. I imagine all the Sapphire agents sitting around, twiddling their thumbs, feeling the same frustration.

Tough. The system is mine for now.

I take a moment to check my phone. Some of my audition buddies have pointed out that it's not midnight to submit your YouTube information to the record label. It's end of business today. EST, same as us. Five o'clock.

I thought I had until midnight!

I glance at the clock.

Crap, it's after four.

I jump to the forums where they've been talking about the submissions.

They are all saying do it by five.

Some are upset, saying the system is slowing down and crashing due to the volume.

Oh no! I need to get mine in!

I glance at the Blue Sapphire screen. It will be fine. The rooms are being held. There are still two under Adolfo Felini.

I will just have to tie up the system a few more minutes.

I jump over to the submission portal for the audition. Like everyone is saying, it's slow to load.

But then I'm in.

Okay.

I quickly type in my name and information, the YouTube channel link, and the link to the video Brady is sending out. I has gotten another fifty views since I last looked.

This is great!

I hit submit with great flourish.

Sam starts packing her stuff. "You staying late?" she asks.

"A little," I say, watching the screen. "I have a couple more things to do."

"See you tomorrow!"

I nod. The little wheel is still spinning.

Then it times out.

No!

I refresh the screen, and now all the boxes are blank! No!

I fill them all in again and hit submit.

Janet starts to pack up.

Shoot!

I minimize the screen so she can't see what I'm doing if she walks by and go back to Blue Sapphire. My heart is pounding.

It still says, "Add new guest?"

I quickly click yes and type in Mitch Roberts.

The system accepts it. His name appears. Then it asks me again. "Add new guest?"

I'm completely relieved. It's all working out.

I type in Brady Wilson, then wait anxiously to see if his money has gone through. This is about the time of day that John's failed yesterday.

But it goes through.

I get one more prompt. "Add another guest?"

That's odd. I should be out of rooms. Maybe there's another one being held for someone else.

But I don't need it. I click the X and close it out.

I did it.

I restore the screen to the Gold Discography

audition form.

And almost faint in relief.

It says, "Submission received."

Janet walks up and I quickly close it out.

"You get those cruise bookings in yet?" she asks.

"I did!" I say. "All three."

"That's some nice money. You'll definitely be our lead agent for the month of January."

"Yay me!" I say.

Janet nods. "You okay to lock up?"

"I am!" I say.

"See you tomorrow." She jingles her keys and pushes out the door.

As soon as she's gone, I slump over on the desk.

Good Lord, that was stressful.

But I did it.

One audition application and three cruises.

Life is looking up.

23: Vivienne

Mitch calls the next day and says an opening came up in his schedule. Would I like another lunch at La Traviata?

But I know the red sofa will be involved after.

He just has to wait. We set up a lunch date for after his return on the cruise so he can clear his schedule ahead. I'm probably a little more descriptive about what I'd like to do on the red sofa that my mama would have appreciated, but his enthusiastic response is worth it.

Thinking about Mitch takes the edge off how I feel when John has to cut our time short to meet with his superior about his next team as a SEAL.

He assures me he'll try to see me before he sets sail. But I book his flight myself and know that he'll be cutting it very close that day, since Blue Sapphire requires everyone on board before noon. I've probably seen him for the last time.

Sigh.

My roommates actually engage with me for once, ordering pizza and having a rom com movie night during the long, empty weekend. Maybe having a boyfriend like John increased my friend value. Which I know is crap and they should like me no matter what.

But I eat the pizza and hang out anyway. I'm not going to die on this particular hill right now.

Everything seems in order for the cruise Monday morning. I have gotten confirmations for all three men and booked their excursions for each port based on what I know about them.

Also to reduce the likelihood that they'll cross paths.

I generally don't know when my clients embark on their adventures, as my part is done.

But Monday morning I have to sit on my hands to avoid biting my nails.

Sam sees me looking all anxious and says, "You think they're going to swap Vivienne stories, don't you?"

"There's thirty cabins," I say. "And they're going

different directions once they get to ports."

"But there is at least one day at sea," she says. "Thirty cabins is what, sixty people? Less?"

"There will be some families."

"Not on Blue Sapphire. And those guys wouldn't be hanging out with them anyway."

She's right. And there's the dining room.

Sam's already thought of this. "How do they handle single travelers for the meals?" she asks. "Let them sit alone or put them together?"

God, I hadn't thought about that. I picture Mitch, Brady, and John at the same table and feel a little faint.

But weren't they all there to see other people?

"I think Mitch has a business contact he'll be talking to," I say. "And John is going to be accosted by someone trying to get him into politics. And Brady is there to convince some casino guy to sponsor him."

Sam runs a file across her dagger nails and blows the dust. "Hopefully none of those people are the same people."

"No way," I say. "I'd know."

She shrugs, and I can't take it anymore. I get up and start organizing the travel brochures on the big rack near the door.

A family walks in, but we send them back to

Janet. Then a well-dressed business woman. I let Sam take her. Business is picking up now that Christmas is well behind and people are spending money again. Spring break fever will hit soon, and everyone will start booking beach getaways.

And I'll have a nice chunk of money from Blue Sapphire to follow my dream a little longer.

And a luncheon with a billionaire. There will be some nice dates. Mitch seems perfectly willing to spend big money. I'll have to buy more fancy dresses.

The phone rings. Since both Janet and Sam are occupied, I rush back to my desk to take it.

The woman on the other end is very curt. "I must speak with Vivienne Carter."

My knees quake a little just hearing her. It's like every mean teacher I ever had and a nurse with the needle all rolled into one.

"Speaking," I say.

"We have a situation aboard the Sea Princess," she says.

"Which cruise line is that?" I ask, sitting down at my desk and quickly bringing up my list of clients on screen.

"Blue Sapphire."

Oh.

"What is the situation?" I ask, my voice shaky

enough that Sam glances over.

A muffled voice in the background says, "I want to know which agent is responsible for this!"

And not quietly.

The woman is muffled next, as if she has her hand over the phone.

I guess she's never heard of "mute."

"I have her on the line," she says.

Then more clearly. "Ms. Carter, we have four men booked in the same cabin."

Oh shit.

But wait.

"I only have three clients aboard!" I say.

"We are well aware, Ms. Carter. Two of them have already arrived."

Oh, geez. Mitch and Brady, most likely. John's flight is just landing.

"Who is the fourth?"

"He is not your client."

Wait. What was the name on that cabin when I added the occupant? My stomach sinks as I realize that cabin really was booked by someone else.

"I think there's been a mix up on your end," I say.

"Mix ups do not happen to Blue Sapphire," she says.

"But there's one now —"

The woman interrupts me. "We need you down at the port immediately or your agency will be stripped of its Blue Sapphire status."

Oh, God. I reach into my drawer and drag out my purse. "I'm coming," I say. "I'll be there in twenty minutes."

"You better be here in fifteen," she says, and the line goes dead.

I set the phone down. "I have to go to the port," I tell Sam, trying to sound calm and confident. There are two other customers here, after all.

"Okay," Sam says with false brightness. "Update me later!"

I push through the door, my heart hammering.

24: Brady the Bull Rider

I'm so ready for this boat.

The whole experience of boarding went smooth as cow's milk. I walked in the door of the port building. Someone already knew my name. I guess that's what Vivienne's picture was for.

They took my bags for me. I was escorted to a fancy room with fabric on the walls and a chandelier over the counter. There they did some security paperwork for the port cities while a funny butler-looking guy in a black suit brought me a breakfast sandwich and orange juice with champagne.

I could live like this.

When all that was done, a chipper young woman escorted me down the deck and onto the boat itself. I had never seen anything like it. Every movie you've ever seen involving a cruise has nothing on this.

Fancy crystal on every table. Flowers all over the place. There wasn't a damn thing that didn't sparkle or shine. All the workers smile and greet you by name. Like they all memorized our pictures.

The girl led me to a room. She called it a stateroom, like this is the White House or something, and showed me where my bags were just inside the door.

And that's when the fireworks started.

Two dudes are already in there arguing with an older lady who is clearly trying to keep her cool. Her big gray beehive shifts back and forth as she nods, trying to placate them.

And one of them is Adolfo Felini! Here I am, just on the boat, and I've already found my mark!

Because I'm pretty fired up about this, it takes me a minute to realize what they're arguing about. Apparently Adolfo booked this room. And so had the business suit dude. Then they notice me.

Adolfo says, "Don't tell me this is your room, too."

I look down at my neatly stacked pair of duffles. They don't fit the fanciness of the room. "That's my stuff."

"I will take care of this," the beehive woman says

and gets on the phone. The girl who brought my bags gets all wide-eyed and backs out slowly. I don't blame her. That other lady looks like she spits lightning.

I'm trying to figure out how to put my best foot forward with Adolfo in this negative situation.

"I'm happy to sleep on the deck," I say. "I've done worse."

That gets their attention. I stick out my hand. "I'm Brady Wilson. I'm a champion bull rider. We sleep outside sometimes. In barns. I'm easy."

Adolfo rolls his eyes and storms out of the room. So that didn't go well.

The other man is a lot calmer and reaches out to shake my hand. "I'm Mitch Roberts," he says. "Apparently there has been a screwup."

"I'm sure they'll handle it. Cutest little gal booked this for me," I say. "She seemed to know her stuff."

"My secretary handled the arrangements," he says. "And she's quite thorough."

"Probably just somebody's X crossed with somebody's Y," I say.

Mitch looks at me for a moment as if trying to figure out what I just said. "Probably so."

Well, this is shittier than a horse stall on Christmas Day.

I reckon they'll figure this out. Since this

probably isn't going to be my room in the end, I don't bother to hang around. I head right on back to the hall to check the place out. Maybe I can talk to Adolfo in a better circumstance. If he storms off the boat, I've spent my life savings for nothing.

My chest tries to get tight with that thought, but I have to let it go. It will work out or it won't. I can't do anything about that part now. What's done is done.

We're on Deck 3, so the sign says. I wander outside and find both the pool and the pool bar.

I figure it's coming up on noon. That's five o'clock somewhere. There's a sharp lookin' fellow behind the bar in a white jacket and black pants. He looks like he's about to go to prom. The people who work here dress a helluva lot better than I do.

I glance down at my flannel and jeans. I should've upped my dressing game.

Too late now. I'm poorer than a church mouse at the moment and don't have much use for suits anyway. The fanciest I get is a pair of khakis when my mama drags me to church.

Good thing I packed them, I guess.

Looking around, I'm not sure how Vivienne got me on this boat at all. I'm not a good fit.

Vivienne.

The thought of her brings me down a notch. I

sure wanted to see that girl again. But I got caught up in Atlanta, then in a tussle in Nashville over the missing check. Still haven't gotten that.

I barely made it back to get on the boat. I don't even want to think about how much it's going to cost to have my truck in that parking garage for ten days.

I sit down on a stool at the bar. The man turns to me. "What can I fix you?"

"Whisky," I say. This is no moment for beer.

"You have a preference?" he asks.

Hell, all the booze here is included. "The best you got," I say.

He nods and turns to the counter behind him. All the shelves are enclosed. Of course they planned for that. Probably we'll go through some choppy waters at some point and the boat will start rockin'.

I look out over the water. There's cruise ships on all sides, most of them ten times the size of this one. But I like it. It's manageable.

A couple comes on deck. The dude wears a white suit and the girl has some fluttery dress with a scarf blowing behind her. They look like a magazine ad.

Hell, I'm really going to look out of place.

The bartender sets the drink in front of me and I knock it back. Only after it's gone do I realize how good it is. Damn, I never had a whisky like that in my life!

"What is that?" I ask.

He shows me the bottle. It's black with a silver crown.

"Royal Salute 32 years," he says.

"That's how old it is?" I ask.

"It is."

Hell, that bottle is older than I am.

"That's some fine drinkin'," I tell him.

He pours me another.

I take my time with this one. I might be liking this rich people vibe now. The couple wanders off and it's just me and this bartender.

"You come alone on the trip?" he asks.

"I have a business partner I'm meeting," I say. "Owns a casino."

"Very nice," he says. "You play cards?"

"Oh no," I say. "I ride bulls."

This gets his attention. "I don't see a bull rider on board very often," he says.

"There aren't that many of us on the circuit."

"That's quite an occupation."

"It is."

I sip the whisky. I wonder how long until we set sail. I should probably keep moving, see if Adolfo is still around.

I finish the drink and push the glass toward the man. "Thank you," I say.

"My pleasure," he answers and takes the glass.

It's a truly fine day outside. The sky is crazy blue and merges into the water. I've never been on a cruise. I'll have to make it worth the life savings it cost me.

Too bad I don't have a woman on it.

This brings me back around to Vivienne.

A sign by the stairs alerts me to a casino on Deck 4. Hmm. That sounds like a real good place to find Adolfo Felini.

I hurry up the steps, now annoyed at myself for wasting time on sun and whisky. I've got ten days for that, but if Adolfo gets off, my chance to impress him is up in smoke.

Everything I pass is fancier than the last. A library with a wall of books and tons of round cushioned chairs. There's not a single spot on this ship that isn't worth more than my entire checking account. Before I blew it all, even.

I see a sign for the casino and duck in.

This room is empty of anyone. It's pretty small. There's a blackjack table and a handful of slot machines. I look around and spot a sign saying that casino operations will begin when the ship is on international waters.

That makes sense. It has to be legal to gamble.

Still, no Adolfo Felini.

Might as well see what's happening in the room. Maybe Adolfo's gone back there. Hopefully they've figured out what's what by now.

25: Mitch the Billionaire

I've put in two calls to Vivienne, but she hasn't returned them. If I'm to understand correctly, the sour-faced lady who called her demanded she come to port.

I hope she isn't in any trouble over this matter. No doubt the cruise line itself screwed up. I won't allow them to make her a scapegoat. All my paperwork was in order, excursions booked, and everyone knew my name when I arrived. As far as I am concerned, she did her part perfectly.

I'm not sad to see her again, though. It's been a long two weeks since we met, and I'm anxious to find out if my second impression will be as favorable as the first.

The insufferable Monte Carlo man has wandered

in and out of the room numerous times. He apparently booked three staterooms on this cruise. The other two rooms are in order, it seems, both couples he is anxious to impress.

Unlike the rest of us. He has been boorish and sullen since he arrived to find me already here. I understand why he doesn't have a lady companion. Who would put up with him?

The woman with the beehive has vacated the room and been replaced with a much more pleasant young lady who brings me tea. We sit together at a small table near the door.

She has springy curls and talks excitedly about her upcoming wedding. She has developed the habit of moving her hands so that her ring shows as much as possible. It's amusing and cute.

"You don't have to entertain me," I say. "I'm more than able to manage on my own."

"Oh," she says, her cheeks pinking up. "I'm required to stay here. You see, there is still one more person assigned to this stateroom. I'm here in case he ends up being escorted by someone who isn't aware of the situation."

"Are there not other staterooms to spread us out in?" I ask.

"No, we are fully booked for this cruise," she

says. "It's possible someone will no-show, which will help. But there are four separate bookings placed here."

"Four. That's quite the mistake," I say.

"It is," she says. "I'm really sorry. Is there anything else I can get you?"

"I'm quite fine," I say.

We sit amicably for a while. I open my attaché and review the Hong Kong contracts. At some point on this cruise, I will have to meet up with the son of the senator who is proposing a bill that will severely damage my dealings with my Hong Kong start-ups.

Negotiations broke down last week, but he seemed to suggest that working with his son would be something that would shift his attention elsewhere. I know an opening when I see it. I'll just have to find this young fellow at some point during the next ten days. With only thirty staterooms, it shouldn't be difficult. From what I understand, he's also traveling alone.

The door opens, and the girl and I look up.

It's the bull rider. Brady, I believe.

He sticks his head in. "They got things sorted out yet?"

The girl stands. "Hello, Brady. From what I understand, the travel agent herself is on her way.

Hopefully we can find an appropriate resolution."

"Vivienne is coming?"

Brady seems rather enthusiastic about the prospect.

"Yes, she is," I say, possibly more harshly than the situation dictates.

We look at each other.

"Is Vivienne your secretary?" Brady asks.

"No, my secretary had Vivienne book the cruise," I say.

The man puffs up a little, like a rooster ready to strut about. "I booked directly with her."

"Well, I met her. She had to do the application," I say.

"Me too," he says.

We eye each other up and down.

And I wonder what transpired between them.

He probably wonders the same about me.

Now her delay in seeing me until after the cruise starts to make more sense. Obviously she needed to throw off this fool.

"When did you last see her?" I demand.

"Three weeks ago," he says. "When I went to her agency."

I relax a bit. He is no threat to anyone.

The casino owner strolls back in. He seems

calmer. Maybe something has been resolved.

"Hear anything?" I ask him.

"No, I've been talking to some of the guests I brought on board," he says. "I'm afraid giving up my spot on the ship isn't an option." He glances at Brady, who has straightened up and put on a more affable expression.

"I'm happy to pull up a cot somewhere," Brady says.

The young woman says, "We do have beds on our rooftop," she says. "Some of our clients like sleeping up there when it's nice out."

"Problem solved," Brady says. "Just spot me a corner somewhere for my bags, and I can be pretty scarce."

"That's very generous of you," the other man says. "What was your name again?"

"Brady Wilson," he says. "I'm a —"

"Bull rider," the man finishes. "I recall that part. Quite a profession."

"It is," Brady says. "Nothing like performing in front of huge crowds on a bucking pile of meat." He extends his hand. Last time the man ignored him. I like that he's not holding a grudge.

This time our errant roommate shakes it. "I'm Adolfo Felini," he says.

"I've heard of you," Brady says. "You manage the best casino in Monte Carlo."

"Have you been there?" Adolfo glances at the bull rider's attire with ill-disguised skepticism.

"I haven't had the pleasure," Brady says, and now he's pouring on the charm. "But your reputation precedes you."

This pleases the man. The two of them head toward the dining table in a small nook off the sitting room. Brady's already forgotten about Vivienne.

That's my cue.

"Can I see my travel agent?" I ask. Of course, as I say it, the image of her naked breasts instantly comes to mind.

The woman checks her phone. "She's arriving on deck right now."

"She's coming to the room?" I ask.

"Apparently."

I close the leather binder and tuck it away. This is a pleasant turn on the day. I have no doubt the room situation will be resolved. Places like this plan for problems.

The door opens, and there she is. I find my throat tightens a bit just seeing her again.

The sour woman with a beehive follows her in.

"I'm so sorry!" Vivienne says when she spots me.

"This is a huge screwup!"

Her hair is all in disarray, curls bouncing. She has on a red dress that fits her perfectly, molded to her ample breasts and flaring at the waist. I want to dance with her just to see it lift in a spin.

"I'm sure it will all work out," I say, reaching for her hands. She lets me take them, then her cheeks go all pink as Brady and Adolfo stop their conversation to look over.

"Viv!" Brady says. "There you are!" He frowns a second at our conjoined hands, then puts on a forced smile.

But I didn't miss it.

"So you recognize the room is mine?" Adolfo asks.

"Unfortunately, it is all four of yours," the pinched woman says. "Ms. Carter booked all of you to this very room."

"Ouch," Brady says. "But I told you, I'm happy sleeping under the stars."

"That's good of you, Mr. Wilson," the woman says. "But our policy is that every guest must have a room prior to reserving one of our *al fresco* beds."

Brady looks confused at the term but keeps his mouth shut.

"Surely you have other rooms," Vivienne says to

her. "Every cruise has cancelations."

"Not every cruise is a Blue Sapphire," the woman says sharply. "We have only ten highly trained agencies and a single-user system for a reason. We fully book, never overbook, and fill every stateroom. There is a waiting list for any cancelations. Even as we stand here, there are two couples in Miami hotels hoping someone doesn't show so they can get on board."

"Oh," Vivienne says. "I sort of remember that now from the training."

"A training you would do well to repeat very soon," she says, "if our company is even interested in doing business with your agency again. Do you realize there are over one hundred agencies hoping for a coveted spot as one of our ten authorized booking partners?"

"Now, that's enough," Brady says. "She messed up. We got that."

"I agree," I add, unhappy that the bull rider came to her defense before I could. "The mistake is past. We should work toward a resolution now."

"I can refund any of you," the woman says. "Vivienne will pay the penalty."

"I will pay the penalty on her behalf," I say. "She worked very hardI'm afraid I'm it was my business in

Hong Kong that delayed my payment and precipitated this mistake."

"Actually, I sent my money in late too," Brady says. "So I was part of the problem."

Vivienne's eyes get teary. "Thanks, both of you, for sticking up for me. But it was my mistake. I saw three rooms with the same name and assumed they were the three Blue Sapphire was holding for me."

I whip around to the beehive woman. "So, the mistake IS yours. You were supposed to hold rooms and you didn't."

The woman's eyes narrow. "It is not our policy to hold rooms for anyone. It is sometimes done as a courtesy for established agencies like Lucky Vega Travel."

She turns to Vivienne. "I will be discussing the matter directly with Lucky herself."

"Lucky's a chick?" Brady asks.

Tears fall down Vivienne's cheeks. "She'll fire me for sure," she says. "I've never been that great of a travel agent."

"Obviously!" the woman says.

"Okay, now, lady, that's enough," Brady says. He steps forward to put his arm around Vivienne. "Don't let this horsehead get you down," he tells her.

"I beg your pardon!" the woman says. The rest of

us try to keep our faces straight. Even Adolfo seems amused by Brady's boorish behavior to defend Vivienne.

Right about then, a porter walks in with another set of suitcases. He's followed by a young man that is the spitting image of the senator I met with in Hong Kong. This could be none other than his son.

He steps in. "Hey, I guess the party's in here!"

"Mr. Jacoby," the sour woman says, forgetting the insult and putting on her first smile of the morning. "So good to see you. Your father has cruised with us so many times."

"Uh, thanks?" He looks around, his eyes lighting up when he sees Vivienne. "Hey, I didn't know you were going to send me off! I ran too late to drop by and see you."

And with that, he walks up and gives Vivienne a long, heavy kiss.

The whole room goes still.

What.

The.

Hell.

26: Vivienne

Oh shit, oh shit, oh shit!

John lays it on thick and heavy right in front of Brady AND Mitch.

My mama is rolling over in her grave. Because I just killed her, and my daddy threw the garden soil over her torn and twisted body.

Even Gramma is shaking her head with a *tut tut tut*.

I break away. "John!" I say. "You made it!"

He tucks my hand under his elbow. "This boat is on fleek!" he says. "I already spotted the jet ski port. Did you know you can take off right from the back of this monster?"

"I didn't," I say. My eyes stay right on his face because I'm afraid to look around the room.

Someone clears their throat.

I don't even want to know who it is. Brady, who untied my green dress in our alternating strip tease? Mitch, who gave me thousand-dollar brandy and drank it out of my belly button?

Or any of the other people in the room who wonder why the crappy travel agent is so tight with the senator's son?

I'm doomed.

I wonder if I'm eligible for unemployment checks.

Probably not. I'm commission based.

God.

I'll have to crawl back to Mama and Daddy. Curl up in the garden with their bones.

So much for Nashville.

"I take it you're the reason three other men are in my stateroom?" someone asks. Someone male.

Time to face the music.

I turn to the voice. It's a tall man, a little darker skinned, with thick black hair. His face is intense, handsome in a twisted way, the sort you'd see in a movie about some tortured character who seduces his captive.

This must be Adolfo Felini.

I let go of John and take a step toward him. "I

am," I say. "It was a terrible mix-up. I was trying to get everyone in the system, and thought three rooms were being held and —"

I stop and turn to the mean lady. She has to be the one who called and demanded I come down. "Wait a minute. Why was I able to even edit Mr. Felini's stateroom? If I had been locked out like all the other bookings, this wouldn't have happened."

Miss Beehive straightens a little. "I have no idea what you're talking about," she says sharply. "And that does not excuse what you did."

I glance over at Adolfo. His lips are pinched tightly together. I'm a little scared of him, actually. He looks like he could eat me.

John comes close again and puts his arm around my waist. "I'm trying to catch up," he says. "Is everyone in here booked to this room?"

"Sort of," I say. "When I got in the system, I entered you and Mitch and Brady. I thought Adolfo was an employee who had held three staterooms for me."

"Which we don't do," the mean woman says again. Like we didn't hear her the first time.

"I'm totally happy to sleep on deck," Brady says.

"Me too," John says. "I hear there's beds up there. Fine by me."

An older man in a flat-topped cap pops his head in the room. "Hilda?" he says. "We need you with the staff."

Her name is Hilda? I have to bite my lip. Is she trying to live up to the witchy name?

Probably I would be a little bitchy if my name was Hilda.

"We haven't resolved this little issue," Hilda says.

"I think we can work it out among ourselves," Brady says.

"Agreed," John says.

"And my offer stands to pay any penalties," Mitch offers.

Hilda looks at all of us for a moment, then rests on John. He obviously has influence over her, as she has quit throwing me shade. "You sure you're all right? I want to make sure you are taken care of."

John squeezes me. "I am."

Hilda presses her lips together again and nods. Then she follows the man out of the room.

The porter and another girl also slip out the door.

Now it's just me and my worst nightmare.

"Looks like this fellow here has some clout with the cruise line," Brady says, sticking out a hand to John. "I'm Brady Wilson, bull rider."

"A bull rider!" John shakes with him firmly. "I

want to hear more about that."

"It's a fun gig," he says. "And there's a killer bar up top."

"That sounds perfect." He turns to me. "You hanging out for a while? Get a drink with us?"

Right. A drink with two men I shagged in January who are already becoming pals. "I think I have to get off the boat soon."

Like before the subject of me comes up.

"All right," John says. "Sure wish you could come along."

He leans down to kiss me, but I keep it short. Mitch is right there, three feet away.

"Have fun," I tell him.

He and Brady take off.

It's hard, but I get up the nerve to turn to Mitch. "Hey," I say.

"Hey," he says back, but it's not a friendly sound. More like he's trying to distance himself.

Which makes sense.

I'm supposed to see him when he gets back. But John sort of claimed me.

Adolfo clears his throat again. "It seems we still have an issue to work out."

I turn to him. Right. The room.

This man seems less menacing now. I guess he

was worried he'd be kicked off or something. Technically, he has the best claim to the room. I hope he won't be unreasonable.

"I'm so sorry this happened," I say. "If the others are willing to take the deck beds, maybe one of you can do the sofa? Alternate?"

It's almost too much to hope that they'll be willing to do that.

"I'll check out these deck beds too," Mitch says. His voice has a bitter edge. "Seems like John Jacoby and I have something in common."

Oh, God. He knows his name.

"Can I take a moment to explain all that?" I ask him. I'm not expecting he'll be okay with it and we'll keep the plans we had. But at least maybe he won't hate me.

"I always give people a chance to say their peace," Mitch says. He stands rigid, his hands clasped behind his back. He looks impeccable in a smart blue suit with his white shirt unbuttoned. Perfect upscale cruise chic.

"I'll let you two have a moment," Adolfo says. He gives us a little nod and strides of out the stateroom.

"Can we sit down?" I ask.

"Sure," he says.

I head to the sofa in the sitting area. This really is a nice room. It's about six times the size of a normal cruise cabin, and more than double the suites I book on the big ocean liners. I've never been on board a Blue Sapphire before.

"This is really nice," I say. I run my hand over the satiny surface of the sofa. There's a wet bar, a dining table, a second sitting area. I cast my eye toward the bed in the partially curtained niche farther down.

Mitch sees where I'm looking and clears his throat. "What did you want to tell me?"

I turn to him. "I'm a whore. A dirty, filthy whore." The shame wave is so big it could knock over this whole boat. "I screwed Brady three weeks ago. Then I screwed you. Then you disappeared and I didn't hear from you for a week. So I screwed John."

"I see." Mitch brushes at the thigh of his suit pants as if there could possibly be a stitch out of place. But it makes me think of his sister's ailing cat and her long white hair that gets everywhere.

"Is Belle okay?"

He seems taken aback by this question. "You remember the cat's name?"

"Of course," I say. "She's a white Persian. And your office is teak and oak. And you gave me Louis the Thirteenth cognac." I look down at my lap. "I remember every detail. Especially the one where you didn't call me."

"I wanted to. I ended up in Hong Kong."

"I know. My office opens at 11 p.m. your time, and closes at 6 a.m. We weren't in good time zones and you didn't have my personal cell."

"You looked," he says.

"I hoped," I say.

Now his hand moves to cover mine. "I should have sent an email. Something."

"You should have," I say.

"Are you in love with John Jacoby?" he asks.

"Oh no," I say. "We just met." But then I think, am I? No, surely not. He's fun. And I like him very much.

"Are you going to keep seeing him?" he asks.

"He's re-enlisting in the Navy," I say. "I didn't expect to ever see him again after today."

"Is that why you wouldn't see me until after the cruise?"

I nod and finally look up at him again. "I wasn't expecting to see you ever again either. I'm used to the good ones never calling me back."

"My Vivienne," he says, and draws me close. "I'm so sorry. We had only just met. I didn't know it would mean so much to you."

245

His lips meet mine, and it's not like it was in his office that day, frenzied and wild. It's gentle, full of promise. My heart turns inside my chest, ever so slowly.

The kiss deepens, and his hand comes to the back of my neck.

I feel like I'm falling into an endlessly deep hole, and Mitch is my only lifeline. I cling to him, our mouths melting together.

He slides me closer to him, turning me so that I'm almost on his lap. His hands move down my back and graze the bottom of my breast. I arch to him and he continues exploring, his hand sliding down my thigh, then up inside my dress.

I'm so lost. This is the best feeling, letting yourself just fall into someone else. I hold on to his suit jacket, rushing with the cascade of emotions, happiness and relief. He's still here. This is still okay.

A long, loud horn blast makes us both jump.

"What is that?" Mitch asks.

"It's the all clear," I say, jumping up. "It means the boat is leaving port!"

I run to the door and jerk it open.

Hopefully it was just a warning!

I race down the hall to the main salon. Shoot, which way was the door to the dock?

I'm momentarily lost. My mind was whirling when Hilda the Evil One dragged me to the stateroom. I can't remember which way to go!

I push through one door but end up in another hall of staterooms. I turn back. I know it was off this big hall full of chairs!

I try the only other door. Outside are two cruise staffers. Thank goodness.

"Where is the ramp?" I ask.

"We've set sail," a young man says. "Can I help you find your room?"

"I'm not supposed to be here!"

The two men look at each other.

"Should we call Hilda?" one asks.

"No!" I say. "No, no. I'm fine. Just lost! Thank you! The salon is back this way?"

"It sure is," the man says, smiling again. "Just let us know if you can't find your way."

Oh, God. I race across the large room filled with chairs and head back to the hall I came from. Are we really gone?

I pass Mitch's room and hurry to the other end. I'm pretty sure that will be the way outside.

Sure enough, a door takes me to the pool deck. Most of the cruise guests are out here, waving back at the port.

And it's true. We've left the dock and are about a hundred yards out.

For a moment, I think of jumping. I'm on a boat that sails for ten days. Nobody knows I'm on board.t.

On this ship are three men I've slept with.

And a man who is pissed I screwed up his room.

And Broom Hilda, who knows I shouldn't be here.

And I don't even have a place myself!

I'm a stowaway.

This makes me laugh.

It's so absurd.

The biggest screwup of my life and what does it get me? A luxury cruise with three hot guys.

And Adolfo isn't so bad either.

Oh my God.

"Gramma," I say, looking up at the sky, which is weird because it's not like she's dead. "You are *not* going to believe what I've done now."

27: John the SEAL

I spot Vivienne hanging on the rail for dear life and elbow Brady. "Did she get stuck on here?"

Brady looks around me and jumps off the stool. "Holy shit. Viv's still on board!"

We leave our drinks at the bar and head over to her. She's got one foot on the rail and looks an awful lot like she's thinking about jumping.

I come up behind her. "I'm into a lot of daredevil things," I say, "but jumping off the side of cruise ship ramping up to full speed is crazy even for me."

She turns her head to me. "I'm so screwed."

I fold myself around her and whisper in her ear, "You bet your sweet ass you are, as soon as I find a suitable spot."

Brady leans against the rail next to us. "Seems like

you two are close," he says. "Been a thing long?"

Vivienne drops her forehead to the rail.

"You okay, baby?" I ask her.

"Just figure it out, you two, okay?" she says.

"What are you talking about?" I ask.

Brady sniffs. "I think she means that she had relations with both of us," he says.

I go still. "When was that?" I ask.

"'Bout three weeks ago."

I relax. "I just met her two weeks ago."

Brady turns to look back over the water. "Then I reckon it's no big deal."

Vivienne doesn't move, so I let her go and take the place beside her on the rail. "It's no big sin to be with more than one guy." I look over at Brady. "Not since then?"

"Nah," Brady says. "I went to Nashville. Just back in this morning."

I push Vivienne's hair off her face. "See, not a huge deal. We're adults here."

She finally looks up. Tears are all down her cheeks. "Y'all aren't mad?"

I let a little laugh out, flashing with a recollection about two years ago on a stand-down when we were one girl short at a party and my pal Ben and I decided sharing was just fine. She was excited at the idea. We had a lot of fun with her. She had a lot of fun too.

"You like your men a little close together?" I ask.

She looks up at me with those honey brown eyes. "It just tends to happen."

I glance up at Brady, who is watching her intently.

"I've done a threesome, so I know a little about what you're feeling," I say.

She rolls her eyes. "I'm sure you could find five girls who'd be willing to go all over you," she says.

"Nah," I say, putting my boot up on the rail. The air is already changing, going all salty and tangy. I breathe it in. "My friend Ben. On my platoon. A girl named Sherry. She sure had a good time with the two of us."

I look up at Brady again. His eyebrows are up, but he's not saying anything against it. "You ever had one, Vivienne?"

She shakes her head.

I thrust my chin at Brady. "What about you?"

"Two girls once," he says. "But I can see the appeal either way."

Vivienne looks at me, then Brady, then back at me. "Is this what you're suggesting?"

"Might be," I say. "I'm all about being free and wild."

She looks at Brady.

He shrugs. "I'm willing to give it a go."

I can't see Vivienne's face, but his eyes meet hers for a long moment.

I'm not the jealous type, not with a girl like Vivienne. I really barely know her. She's been my ticket to some great experiences, on cliffs and in the ocean, and with her too. I won't forget that balcony any time soon.

I'm totally down for anything. I don't care who's involved, as long as they aren't jackasses. This Brady guy is cool as shit. A bull rider. I'm going to have to have a go at that some time. He already said he could get me on one. Now that's some insider stuff right there.

But right now, I'm all about Vivienne.

"You think those other two are in the room?" I ask.

Vivienne sucks in a breath at that. "I don't know." Her voice is a little strained. I get that. She might not want everybody and their dog knowing she's up to a little bit of naughty.

"There's the rich dude right there," Brady says. "He's belly up to the bar."

Vivienne turns. "Mitch," she says.

"What's his name?" I ask.

"Mitch Roberts," she says.

Bloody hell, that's the guy my dad insisted I meet up with. I guess that'll be easy, with him right in the room.

But business later. Vivienne now.

"Looks like he's occupied," I say. "If the other guy isn't in there, we're good to go."

Getting Vivienne back in the sack has become a necessary item on my immediate agenda.

But she hesitates. "I don't know."

"I never knew Vivienne to back away from some wild fun," I say.

I pull her off the rail.

She glances back at Mitch a moment.

And I get it.

"You been with him too?" I ask.

Her look is a little tortured as she turns her face back to me.

"Shit, Viv!" Brady says. "You got the whole client list on your chain!"

"Let me tell you a little secret," I say to her, my face close to her ear. "We don't give a fuck."

And I pull her along.

Brady starts singing a little song, "Vivienne Carter naked in a tree, f-u-c-k-i-n-g."

This makes her laugh, so I join in with my terrible

out-of-tune voice.

"First comes Brady," I say.

"Then comes John," Brady says.

"Then the whole cruise boat joins along!"

She's in stitches by the time we get to the stateroom on Deck 3.

And guess what?

It's empty.

28: Vivienne

Well, I done killed my whole family dead with my terrible deeds.

At least, I will have if they find out about it.

So I might as well live it up.

Brady has me by one hand and John's got the other.

This is without a doubt the craziest thing I've done in my life.

Will ever do.

I can't believe they want it.

Want me.

Both of them.

At.

The.

Same.

Time.

Case in point number ten: I've seen porn. I know the logistics. I've got two holes back there. And a mouth.

But I have never in my living days used more than one at a time.

I don't even know what to expect.

We're no more in the door when Brady is tugging at my dress, pulling the zipper down the back.

John chucks my purse on the sofa as we pass it.

By the time we get to the little nook with the bed, Brady's got the dress off and John is unfastening my bra.

Brady turns me around and the world becomes a blur as I fall backwards on the bed.

They're like two wolves on prey. I can barely keep track of what's happening. Brady's up top, kissing me, his hands cupping both boobs.

John is down below, inching my panties down, knocking off my shoes.

The word devoured comes to mind as four hands and two mouths take over my body.

Brady has a nipple between his teeth, the intensity of it making my hips rise in the air. John takes advantage of this position, holding me up and spreading my knees.

His tongue slides into me, and I'm blissed out. I've never even thought it could be like this. So many points of pleasure. I'm overwhelmed.

Brady pulls off his shirt and now I have something to do, touching his muscled chest. We keep kissing until John draws my attention again. I suck in a small gasp and Brady quirks a cute smile. "I know that sound," he says.

John's pace picks up, his fingers delving into me, cruising along that G-spot.

Brady trails his mouth along my shoulder, my collar bone, and down to a breast again.

And I lose it, hard, crying out, lifting into John, clutching Brady. My words echo in the tiny room, names, jumbles of syllables. My body shudders until I sink back down onto the silky bedspread.

"Nice start," Brady says.

John withdraws slowly, setting my legs carefully down. He jerks his shirt off, and the sight of both of those killer man-bods is enough to make me want to swoon.

Brady shucks his jeans and boxers, and John laughs and races to beat him.

Then they're both in front of me, dicks out.

"One at a time or shall we try both?" Brady asks. He elbows John. "You're the expert."

"It's all about Vivienne," John says. "We never tried any anal together. You game?"

"Can we work up to that?" I ask. "I tried it before but it was sort of clumsy."

Both men say at the same time, "We can fix that."

Then they laugh and shove on each other.

"Boys," I say, like I'm their babysitter, then the idea makes me giggle. We all get a good long laugh and Brady sits on the bed beside me and rolls me on my belly.

John grasps my hips so I'm up on all fours.

"I hope you guys brought a shit ton of condoms," I say.

"We did," they both say at the same time, and there's another round of laughter.

"Even so," Brady says, "I bet you can order them on room service. They've got everything."

He searches around for his jeans and pulls one out of his wallet. John drags me to the edge of the bed.

"John, come over here," I say.

"Yes, ma'am."

I pull him close, running my hands along those abs that I love so much, fingers trailing through the indentions that lead from his hips down to that cock that is totally standing at attention.

I hold on to it and drag him even closer, then take that throbbing length of him into my mouth.

The bed shifts as Brady closes in behind me. Nice. I'm glad he's going in first since we didn't even do the official deed the night we met.

I run my tongue up and down John. He grabs my head, digging his fingers into my scalp. His eyes are closed and he looks beautiful.

Brady slips his fingers inside of me, his palm flush against my skin. "You're so wet," he says.

You bet I am.

Then something thicker and longer fills me up. A glorious shiver of pleasure zips through my body. I take John deeper into my mouth and he lets out a groan.

Brady takes it easy at first, and the three of us move together. John's hands reach down to cup my breasts, then Brady takes a hand around front to massage my clit.

I'm losing my mind.

John in front of me. Brady behind. I'm so lost. It's overwhelming, the sensation, the emotions.

I want to feel this forever, the attention, the pleasure, the absolute wantonness.

John pulls back and crawls across the bed near

Brady.

"I'll show you a little trick," he says.

I look behind me. "What are you two doing back there?"

"It's none of your concern," John says with a laugh.

Brady slows down. They whisper conspiratorially, then John heads to the other room.

Brady takes his time, sliding in and out, going easy on me, one hand still between my legs and the other reaching for a breast. "You are amazing," he says.

I'm something, that's for sure.

John returns with a small bottle. "We'll take care of you just fine, Vivienne," he says.

Oh boy.

Brady pulls out and slides beneath me. We're face to face and he kisses my nose. "You ready for this?" he asks.

I nod. Brady slips inside me again, now from below.

John closes in behind. Then I feel a finger slipping inside my butt.

I tense up for a moment, but several hands start massaging me.

"Just relax, love," John says, and the endearment

alone makes me take a long exhale.

I take deep breaths, and Brady picks up his pace. I move into him, relishing the feeling of him filling me up.

Then John goes in again, and this time, slips inside.

The burst of intense pleasure surprises me, and I suck in a breath.

"That's it," John says. "Just feel it."

Now I'm losing my mind again, wanting more, moving ahead of Brady, picking up the pace.

Both boys follow my lead, speeding up. John spreads me a little wider.

"Lean back a little," John says. I look back and have to smile at him behind me. And I feel it as he pushes the tip of his cock inside.

Brady moves hard against me from below while John takes his time. The sensation of both of them inside me is wild. I feel dizzy, like the world has started spinning.

When John starts his movement, I lean down and groan into Brady's chest. This is sex on steroids. I grab great handfuls of the comforter on either side of Brady.

The two of them sync their pacing and it's all I can do to hang on.

It's like lightning striking in two places at once. Brady picks up speed again, and John shifts to keep up. My body is humming like I am electric, little shocks of intense pleasure sparking through me at random.

When the orgasm begins, I can't even figure out where it comes from. Everything is in the zone. My muscles are tense. Every ounce of blood is beating through my heart at once.

When I start to cry out, pushing against them both, driving them deeper, Brady loses it first. The pulsing sets off another round of contractions inside me. I'm crying and laughing and hiccupping. It's so intense.

John works me through it, taking it easy, and when I come down, he drives in again. Brady uses his arms to support me.

"One more for us, Viv," Brady says. "You got one more?" One of his hands slides along my breasts and belly to rest between my legs.

"I don't know," I say. I'm so tired and wrung out.

But Brady finds that good spot, and John keeps an easy, seductive pace.

I lean my head on Brady's shoulder and feel that spark firing up again. I don't see how, but it's doing its own thing. It wants more.

I rest fully on Brady, just surrendering to everything, the exhaustion, the pleasure, the newness.

And from that total submission comes a different sort of pleasure. It's like an ache that gently shifts into a need, heavy and widespread.

My body moves on its own, finding a rhythm between us. And the notes begin to play, like the sexiest love song, starting slow but becoming more urgent.

Energy comes from nowhere, a second wind. John holds me by the hips, following my lead.

Brady keeps his fingers working.

This one is so different, like thunder rolling. I don't have words this time, just groans, letting the dark, intense pleasure take over.

John holds still, and I'm vaguely aware of the throbbing as he releases into me. Brady squeezes tightly, hanging on to the moment.

The world stops, then tilts, and finally it all lets go.

I think I'll scream, but my voice is gone, and only a long, strangled cry escapes. John holds me, and Brady supports me, so when I crash in on myself, they ease me down to the bed.

The covers move, and I slide across cool sheets.

Someone smooths my hair away from my face,

and lips press into my forehead.

Then I'm covered, tucked in. The solidness of two warm bodies presses in on both sides.

I don't know how much time has passed, but it feels like night, and I completely drift away to sleep.

29: Mitch the Billionaire

I have no idea where Vivienne went. If she made it off the boat.

I walk the ship, learning the decks, imagining her in the red dress at every beautiful spot. I should have insisted she come with me. Working girl, she said. I could have done anything. Put her on my payroll. Paid off her house, whatever she needed.

But Vivienne is independent. I can see that.

I get a drink by the pool, visit the library and the tiny casino. A few other guests mill the open spaces, looking happy and relaxed.

There's a bar at the tip top of the yacht, and I spot the outside beds that were mentioned. If the weather's nice, it will be fine to sleep up here.

I sit on one of the cushioned chairs, trying to

relax into the idea of a vacation. It will be awkward negotiating with John Jacoby since he was with Vivienne all this time. I suppose I can corroborate that he is going back to the Navy.

Except that one of the reasons I'm here is to convince him to follow in his father's footsteps instead.

And if I succeed, he won't re-enlist and will be free to pursue Vivienne.

I'm going to have to let go of her. Just set aside this infatuation. Life is business. My business is my life.

A waiter pauses and asks if I'd like another brandy. Amazing service here. My last brandy was ordered at another bar three decks down from a completely different staffer. They can get that right, and yet still somehow end up with four separate bookings in the same stateroom.

"No, thank you," I say automatically, then hold out my hand. "Actually, yes. I would."

This is as good a time as any to drink my problems away.

The afternoon has dwindled by the time a young woman lets me know it's an hour until the formal dinner and asks if I'd prefer a seating in the dining room or dinner in my quarters.

Since the suite is being shared, I choose the dining room. I also request John Jacoby be seated with me if he is amenable. She says she will check.

Might as well get started on that.

I make my way down to Deck 3 so I can change into dinner attire. This cruise, which was initially just a necessary nuisance for a greater purpose, is now a major pain in my life. I'll just have to grit my teeth for ten days around this man.

The room has been darkened when I arrive. The draperies are closed and lights dimmed.

I feel around for a switch and turn on a light in the sitting room. With the lights out, at least I know I'm alone.

Across from the dining nook is a long closet. I open it and find all four of our luggage stuffed inside. I guess they weren't sure whose to unpack, so they left them all.

Only two suit garment bags are hanging. By the looks of the four of us, I'm sure the other is the casino gentleman's. Neither the bull rider nor John seems as though they care much for formalities.

I pull a black suit from the bag, as well as a tie. Tonight is less formal than some of the other nights, where a tuxedo will be more appropriate. I flip on the bathroom light and am about to step inside when I sense a movement from the bed.

The light barely reaches the little nook. I walk over to one of the small lamps and feel along the base until I find a switch.

Then catch my breath.

The tender light falls on the tangled covers, a disarray of honey red hair, and a glorious naked breast that I would know anywhere.

Vivienne.

She's still on the yacht!

I sit next to her.

Is she waiting for me?

Then I remember.

John Jacoby.

She stirs a little, shifting on the bed. She must be warm now, as she pushes more of the bedding aside.

Her skin is luminous, golden and rosy. I should walk away, but I am powerless to resist. I push an errant curl away from her face, then trail my fingertips down her cheek, her shoulder, and alongside the soft, wondrous breast.

Her eyes flick open. When she sees me, she sits up quickly.

"Mitch!"

"You're still here," I say.

"I am." She glances around. "It's just you?"

And I realize, yes, John was here with her. That's why she is naked.

"You were expecting the senator's son?"

She closes her eyes. "Yes, no. I don't know. I was so tired." She presses a hand to her belly, like it aches.

"No reason why you can't wait for him here." I move to leave, and she reaches out to hold my wrist.

"No, it's fine," she says. "I need to tell you something."

"I can see that you have been with John. It's fine. I know when to step aside."

Her throat bobs with a hard swallow. "But I don't want you to."

Her skin is warm on mine. She looks so lovely lying there, like a classic painting. Renoir perhaps. One of the old masters.

And I realize, this is what will make the cruise endurable. Her. Maybe she will sleep with that other man too. Maybe she is nothing I can keep for long.

But she's here.

And I want her.

I lean forward, and she moves toward me. Our lips meet, and her soft, glorious body is so close. My hands need to touch her and move along her skin. I feel ravenous, desperate. The ache is intense.

She shoves aside the covers and I can see all of

her, beautiful, all woman. She gets to her knees and pushes my jacket off my shoulders.

I allow her to undress me, piece by piece.

She kisses her way along each part of my newly exposed skin. My chest, my belly, shoulders, arms.

I stand, and she unbuckles my pants and lets them fall. Then my boxers, down, out of her way.

When she takes me in her mouth, I hold her head, exultant, feverish.

She is mine.

I must have her.

I push her back on the bed.

She falls onto the pillows.

I want to own her, possess her. The need of her is wild and intense.

The anger is there too. Anger that she cannot be simply mine. That there are impediments, and it's all mixed up. My business deal. That senator's son. And her.

My hands take her wrists and pull them above her head. Her breasts move high and taut. I feast on one, moving my body over hers.

The tie is still on the bed, so I grab it and wind it around her wrists. I don't know if she will like this, but she moans and arches her back. So she does.

I'm raging with my want of her now. I quickly

lash her arms to the slats of the headboard.

Now her body is mine to do with as I please. Not John Jacoby's.

Mine.

I spread her legs. I want inside her. There will be no waiting.

She's slick and wet and I easily glide inside.

She arches again, and those luscious breasts are too tempting to resist. I bend down, taking one on my mouth while kneading the other.

I start slow, relishing the feel of her surrounding me. I realize I've forgotten the condom. "Will I need to pull out?" I ask.

She shakes her head no.

I straighten and grasp her legs, pulling her ankles to my shoulders.

Nothing will slow me down now. I pump into her with unrelenting speed and power. The mattress rocks beneath us, and she grips the rails near her bound hands.

Her moans become gasps and I can feel her tightening around me. She calls out my name, and God, and Jesus, and I have to smile, remembering our time in my office.

I press hard, each thrust another glorious rise into the big finish.

"Yessss," she says. "Yes, yes."

The pressure builds, and I grasp her hips, then release into her.

The unleashing of all this tension and emotion is like a dam breaking. I let her legs down and hold tight, pressing deeply inside her, feeling the spasms that pump my seed into her. I imagine her getting pregnant and feel elated at her being mine, belly swollen with my child.

Mine.

Her breathing is fast. I reach up and release her wrists.

Her arms drop to the bed, and I massage her skin. "It didn't hurt you, did it?" I ask.

She shakes her head no.

I pull her against me, warm and soft and feminine.

I won't let her go. No matter what is going on with John.

But I must know how things stand.

"Were you with him earlier?" I ask.

She nods. She looks up at me with bright beautiful eyes.

"Do you regret being with me now?" I ask.

She shakes her head. Her hand comes up to my jaw. I sense in her all the emotion she does not seem to want to express.

"I can live with this if you can," I say.

She opens her mouth, then closes it. Then presses her face into my chest.

"I know you're not a traditional girl," I say.

Maybe this is the only way I can have her. But I can't let her go.

"There's more," she says, her mouth moving against my skin.

I tighten my arms around her. "More what?"

"Brady too," she says quietly. "I met him first."

"Before the cruise?" I ask.

She nods. "And today."

"You were with both of them today?"

She nods.

I hold on to her. Okay. I will have to adjust my view. I can be open minded. I won't judge her. None of us are married or lying or cheating.

Just enjoying her.

"It's okay," I tell her. "It's all right."

She hangs on to me. "I never imagined myself here," she says.

"Me neither," I say.

There's a knock at the stateroom door. "Dinner," a man announces.

Shoot. It's time? I'll skip.

But then the door opens.

"Thanks for taking care of this," says another voice. It's that bull rider!

"This looks great," says another. John!

They are both in the room?

Vivienne looks at me, her eyes wide.

I slide on my boxers and slip on the shirt. Vivienne looks around for her dress, fails to spot it, and wraps up in the sheet.

We head down the short hall.

Brady and John are sorting through several trays of dishes covered in silver domes. They look up when they see us.

"Hey, love birds," Brady says. "We got dinner for you both. Hope you don't mind eating in here. Had to cancel your formal dining."

"How long have you been in here?" I demand.

"Long enough," Brady says with a laugh. He elbows John. "Billionaire here got a solo turn."

"I was totally cool with the threesome," John says. He winks at Vivienne. "You feeling all right, baby?"

I glance down at Vivienne. "Both at once?" I ask.

She bites her lip.

Well.

"Hungry?" Brady asks. "I bet you two are."

"We had to go get burgers at the grill while we waited on this," John says. "Did you know you can get pretty much anything you want cooked any time you want it here? I should have done a cruise before!"

I sit down on the padded bench and pull Vivienne beside me. John and Brady take the two chairs.

"This looks good," Vivienne says. "I am pretty hungry."

We dive into the food, pork loin and garlic mashed potatoes and tender asparagus. John starts feeding Vivienne, and it gets to be a game. I'm uptight about it all at first, but then Vivienne feeds me. Vivienne drinks wine and the rest of us drink brandy, although John takes some coaxing with Vivienne telling him to lick it off her.

And by the time we're done with food, everyone's sort of sprawled out and Vivienne has agreed to lose the sheet so we can all admire her.

I'm definitely in new territory.

30: Vivienne

I've never felt more like a goddess.

Yeah, I'm naked in a stateroom with three men. We're doing some crazy stuff. Our cell service quit working an hour ago, except Mitch's and his fancy satellite feed. The rest of us agreed to skip the on-board wi-fi and started using our phones to take wild video we'd never dare while we had signals.

Brady videoed John eating mashed potatoes off my nipples.

Then John took shots of Brady drawing an arrow with raspberry sauce from my belly pointing down. Then licking it off.

Licking things off my body has become standard. Brady and John have sworn off plates for the duration of the cruise.

Mitch has mostly watched the antics, but he's smiling more than usual. We're laughing and drinking, and I'm just letting go of everything.

John squeezes my thigh and I let out an "Oh!"

"I'm sore!" I say, thumping him on the arm. "Look what you guys have done to me!"

"We have a solution for that!" John says. "Hot tub!"

"I don't have a suit!" I say. "In fact, I don't have anything!"

"We'll take care of it," Mitch says. "I'll call down to the boutique."

And sure enough, twenty minutes later, two ladies show up with a whole rack of clothes and bathing suits.

I want the black and white retro one-piece, but John insists on a red micro bikini.

Mitch gets them both.

Everyone agrees on a backless yellow sundress and cute flower flip flops.

I pick out a couple pair of shorts and a strapless halter top as well as an ordinary T-shirt, which I'm sure is crazy expensive even though it's something you could get at Wal-Mart.

Then we spot the red sequined gown.

"That's it," Brady says. "It's perfect."

"Go put it on, Vivienne," John says.

So I do. When I come out, John and Brady whistle.

"Now that's the ticket," Brady says.

"You got any lingerie?" John asks.

The woman, to her credit, doesn't bat an eye that I'm sitting there with three men. She reveals an adorable pink baby doll with a ruffly hem, a red one-piece that is missing three critical spots, and a sheer black shortie robe.

"All of it," Mitch says.

The women leave it all behind. I'm sorting through my new things when John comes up behind me. "Into that red micro, darling. We're headed to the hot tub."

I glance up at him. "Everyone?"

John extends his arms. "Everyone."

Oh, boy.

We wait until after dark. Everyone seems to be on Deck 6 where they're having a Bon Voyage party with live music.

The hot tub is empty.

"Take off that robe, darlin'," Brady says. "You haven't shown us that bikini yet."

The shame wave is threatening. I do not have a body for micros. Too much boob. Too much thigh.

Too much everything. And pale to boot. It's like I'm a plucked chicken tied with string. I'm not in the stateroom any more.

Mitch and Brady have on board shorts while John, as you might figure, is wearing a tiny navy blue speedo. All of them look spectacular.

I clutch the robe to me. "Make sure the water's hot," I say.

The night *is* a little chilly.

"Look at the steam coming off," John says. "It's fine." He jumps in with a splash. "Feels great."

Brady hops in after him, not taking his eyes on me. Mitch takes the steps and settles on the circular seat.

Looking at the three of them, sweat already beading on their foreheads, I have a terrible case of insecurity. They're going to see me in this thing and wonder what the hell is so great about me. They'll turn me in to Broom Hilda and she'll make me ride on an inflatable raft behind the boat.

"We're waiting," Brady says. "And I already got my dick in my hand."

John splashes him in the face.

"Give her time," Mitch says.

I glance around. There's no one other than a bartender on the other end of the deck. It's so dim over here, just a low blue glow around the rim of the tub, I doubt he can even see us. The guys are mostly in shadow, even this close.

I take a deep breath. All these men have seen me naked and still got it on just fine. I need to be bold. Have confidence. Toss that shame wave over the rail.

So I drop the robe to the deck.

Every last one of those men suck in their breath.

I guess that's good.

My gaze rests on each of them in turn as I slowly walk to the edge of the hot tub and dip my toe in. It feels marvelous.

Their eyes follow me as I slowly step into the water.

"Damn," Brady says.

"I'll say," John adds.

"Come here," Mitch says. "Sit by me."

I remember him tying me to the bed and my heart beats a little faster. But I do as he says and sit beside him.

Brady scoots along the bench closer to me.

John slides down to the middle of the tub. His body wavers beneath the water.

"I believe we promised to help those muscles," he says. His hands reach out and grab my ankle. He squeezes my foot, turning it left and right, and starts making his way up my calves.

I close my eyes and let my head fall back onto the padded wall behind me. It feels soooo good.

Another pair of hands start massaging my arm. Brady, judging by the location.

Then another kneads the back of my neck. Mitch.

A girl could get used to this.

John's hands make their way up to my knees, then my thighs. He spreads my legs to get access to more muscles. My eyes pop open to watch him float in front of me, hands on my body.

Brady lifts me and slides behind so I sit in his lap. His hands cup my bottom. "How is this?" he asks, his mouth next to my ear, as he squeezes.

"Perfect," I say.

I turn to Mitch. He kisses me, his lips soft and gentle. Are we going to do something here? In the open? With all of them?

The sounds of the party on the upper deck spill down. The bartender at the pool bar cuts out his lights and walks back to the interior of the ship.

We're alone.

I kiss Mitch a little more urgently. All three of them sense my engagement, and their hands on my body shift from massage to caress.

It's bliss. The warm water. The stars. These men.

The bikini is so small, it doesn't even have to come off. Mitch slides the tiny triangle off one breast and lowers his head to take a nipple in his mouth.

Brady rocks beneath me, his hard cock pressing up, his hands on my waist.

John slips his thumb beneath the narrow base of the bikini bottom. When he finds the nub, I sink back into Brady, grinding against him.

Brady groans. "That's it," he says.

Mitch pulls my knee wider to make it easier for John to reach me. God, they're working together.

Brady shifts, and I feel the rigid length of him directly against my skin. "May I?" he asks, and I know he means without the condom.

"Yes, *please*," I whisper.

Brady shifts me, and John pulls the bottom of my bikini out of his way. For a moment, I float in the water, away from Brady's lap. Then he pulls me down.

His cock splits me wide. I gasp, clutching Mitch's hand. He gives me his arm for leverage.

"That's gorgeous," John says, pushing both parts of my bikini top aside so that my breasts bob on the water.

I clutch at Mitch as Brady holds my waist, lifting me up and slamming me down on his cock, over and over again. The water shifts and moves around us, splashing lightly against the lip of the tub.

So many sensations are new. The gentle sweep of warm water over my body. The touch of so many hands and thighs and lips.

The orgasm is deep down, tight, and fast. I push into Brady and the others help me until the water rolls like a wave.

When I start to cry out, John captures my mouth, taking the sound into himself. Brady holds me still, and I feel the warm rush of him fill me. I've never not used condoms until Mitch this afternoon. And now Brady. Thank goodness I'm on the shot or who knows whose baby I would end up with.

Brady squeezes my arms and lifts me away.

"How are you feeling?" John asks, pulling me against his body.

"Amazing," I say.

"You up for more amazing?"

I wrap my legs around him. "Always."

He reaches between us and drops his Speedo just enough to let his cock spring free. His finger slides inside me. "Oh, you are so warm and ready."

I wrap my arms around his neck. "I am."

He reaches down and slides his dick against me. "I'm safe," he says.

"I trust you," I tell him.

And in it goes, thick and hard. He kisses me and takes us in circles along the base of the tub. We float together, letting the movements set the pace.

It's gentle and sweet, and for a moment my eyes smart with emotion. We pass Brady and Mitch, both watching us. I feel so wild, so free, so crazy. I think I'm falling for them all. I like them all individually, but together, they are overwhelming.

I release my arms and float on my back, still joined to John. My hair swirls around me and I stare up at the stars. The chill makes my nipples tighten. Mitch approaches and slides beneath my head, holding me against his chest. His hands cup my breasts, keeping them warm.

I feel like a goddess again, protected and loved by my…what? Consorts? Slaves? None of those seem right.

Then I know.

My harem.

I'm like the Sultan. And they service me.

Except they get what they want too.

John's pace speeds up. He holds my thighs, and the water starts to shift and move.

"There it is," Brady says. He runs his hands along my belly, circling down and holding up my lower back. It helps, and I'm exerting almost no effort as

John plunges in.

Mitch reaches for my clit and rubs in tiny circles. This is just the extra bit I need, the sparks starting to fly from where John works me over.

Brady takes the mouth duty this time, absorbing my cries. John groans, working straight through the pulsing, and I'm filled with warmth again. I thrust against him, drawing out my own contracting muscles. How can someone survive this many orgasms in one day?

John withdraws, and Mitch catches me as I sink down. He turns me to face him and sits on the bench, cradling me against his chest.

"Damn," John says, shaking water from his short hair. "This is already one helluva cruise."

Mitch just holds me against him, fingers smoothing my wet hair. "Just rest," he says to me. "It's been a lot today."

I curl into him, spreading my knees to fit more comfortably against his body. I'm relaxed and warm and happy. The water settles and the night sounds filter in again. The party above is starting to wane. A random couple walks farther along the deck, stands at the rail for a moment, then heads inside.

I still have on the bikini, and from the back, the tie makes it look normal. Mitch and I are just a couple cuddling, and John and Brady are friends.

Everything is fine.

John finds the button for the bubbles and they laugh that they didn't figure it out before. Brady says he'll steal a soda can from the bar to toss in to ensure they clean the hot tub well before tomorrow.

I stay snuggled in Mitch's arms, reveling in the beautiful night, the easy friendship of the two other men, and the caress of the moving water.

I shift position again, taking pressure off my knees, and feel Mitch's hard cock brush my belly. He's taken care of everything I've needed today. The room. The clothes. He's accepted this situation when he wanted me for himself.

I reach between us and slide my hand along the length of him. He takes in a breath. "You've had a lot today," he says.

I lean into his ear. "Can I have one more?"

His cock is inside me in an instant. His speed and precision take my breath away.

The others stop fooling around to turn and watch us.

"Nice," Brady says.

Mitch holds my hips, and we work together, fighting the buoyancy of the water to collide over and over again.

John comes over and helps, holding me against him to give me leverage. My breasts sway on the water, and I can't take my eyes off Mitch. He stares at me with such intensity and lust.

Just his look alone sends a shock of heat through my body. It's clear how much he wants me, how necessary I am. I clutch his arms and give it all I have, forcing myself down through the water and deeper against him.

His control is merciless, his expression unchanged, and I'm determined to break him, to make him crumble. I lean forward, my breasts in his face, slamming down. John glides away, and I hook my legs behind Mitch, grinding against him, barely able to breathe.

And he lets out a groan. His arms clutch me. I slam down on him again and again. His arms tighten, then he's lost. I've done it. His face is buried in my chest, his cock pulsing inside me. I don't even care that I didn't orgasm again. I wanted this. I wanted him to lose it when I chose, not when he did.

He doesn't move for long moments. I hold him tight against me. Someone else walks by, too close, and I know my breasts are exposed, Mitch's face between them, but I don't care. I'm sure all sorts of crazy happens on these cruises. It's just boobs.

Mitch takes in a deep breath and lifts his head. I don't bother to fix the bikini. Let the other person look. It doesn't matter.

"I thought about you the whole time I was gone," he says. "I could not bear to let you go."

I pull him in tight again, my head on his shoulder.

Brady and John sit off to the side, watching and nodding. Then Brady looks behind us. "Hey, it's our roomie! Yo, Adolfo!"

The man steps forward, and I stick close to Mitch so that the state of my bathing suit isn't obvious.

"Good evening," he says, looking down at us. "I see the travel agent is still with us."

I reach between me and Mitch and straighten out the bikini. Then I sink down below the bubbles so that only my head shows.

I look up to him. "The boat sailed before I could get off."

"You seem…close to your clients," he says. He stands tall over the hot tub, extremely well dressed in a black suit and red tie. I feel practically naked next to him.

Well, I sort of am.

"She is," Mitch says. "We'll be sleeping up on Deck 6," he says. "So you can have the room for the night."

"Very well," he says. "I've been entertaining my guests. It has been no inconvenience."

"Thank you," I say. "For helping us out."

He looks down at my face, taking in my shoulders, the top of my cleavage, going in and out of view with the movement of the water. I sink a little more.

"You are very lovely," he says. "I can see why they are taken with you."

And with a nod, he walks on.

"Damn, that's one slick willy," John says.

"Let's stay on his good side," Brady says. "I need him, remember."

"Whatever for?" Mitch asks.

"Sponsorship," John says. "Bull rider here is ready to take it to the next level."

"Interesting," Mitch says. "Well, we'll try to maintain good relations."

They are being awfully reasonable.

"Should we go figure out the beds?" I ask.

"Absolutely."

"Of course."

"Yes, ma'am."

They help me out of the hot tub and back into my robe. We set back out for the room, dry clothes, and hopefully before too long, a place to sleep.

31: Adolfo from Monte Carlo

The cruise is going according to plan, despite the inconvenience of four unexpected roommates.

The whole lot of them are carrying on in the sitting room this morning as they change into bathing suits, so I step outside to the poolside deck to get away from the noise and frivolity. I have business to attend to, and the crude lot of them are a distraction.

We have a day at sea, which benefits me as I can continue to woo the guests of the ship, both the ones I brought aboard and the others, and encourage their patronage to my casino. I've had too much low-end tourism of late and not enough of the type of client that keeps my establishment at the top of every profit margin.

On a cruise like this, everyone is the right sort of

client.

I have my particular eye on the businessman who got caught up in the saucy travel agent's error. I've checked up on him. Mitch Roberts. His net worth could actually buy out my casino. He seems a bit serious and uptight, or he did at first meeting. Since the three of them have been gallivanting with that girl, he has relaxed considerably.

I sit at the poolside bar and order a scotch. Several couples are frolicking in the pool. I watch their easy romance and wonder why other men find it so easy to associate with women. It has always been a source of great stress and discomfort to me.

Back in Monte Carlo, I have resorted to enlisting the aid of a very exclusive and discreet escort service to ensure I have a date of proper elegance and stature for important social engagements. Most of them are willing and perfectly agreeable to take the evening to a carnal conclusion, for a fee.

It has been enough.

I paid a psychologist a rather handsome sum to determine the root of my issue, why having a woman who was not paid to be in my company caused me such duress. Five figures later, I fired him for concluding the fault was with my mother and I just needed to find "the one" to fix it.

I am not an American, and I did not ask for Dr. Phil.

So here I am, watching romance from a distance. I didn't bother hiring someone to be with me for this voyage. I guess I followed the psychological quack to some extent, hoping that somehow I would "get lucky."

It's just as well I don't have a lady guest, since my stateroom has been overtaken by an orgy. I saw them in the hot tub last night. The travel agent was servicing that wealthy man right there in public. And by the looks on the other two men's faces, they were expecting their turns as well.

I did not lie when I said she was lovely. She is. But I do not understand their motives for sharing one woman, or her, for taking on the three of them.

The whole lot of them stumble out onto the deck. The girl wears an old-fashioned black and white bathing suit. Which, I admit, suits her well. They laugh, even the stoic businessman. What sort of witchery is she up to? Gold digging, no doubt. Or covering for her egregious error.

They spot the number of people in the pool and act more soberly. At least they can behave in a crowd. I tap the bar for a second drink and observe them. I spoke to the Brady fellow quite a while yesterday. He seems to be wheedling for some sort of endorsement from my casino. He's brought up the Formula One racing more than once and made comparisons to his bull riding.

I've never witnessed this *rodeo*, as he calls it. It sounds dreadful, all stomping animals and dust. But I will look into it.

The four of them splash around for a bit, then take off for elsewhere. I down the drink, thank the bartender, and decide to follow them. My curiosity about this strange dynamic is too strong.

They head into the bowels of the boat to where the staff stores all manner of jet ski, raft, canoe, and other aquatic diversion.

The senator's son, John, is broad as a barn. He argues that he has done diving off a moving vessel numerous times and seems rather put out that the staff won't let him water ski off the back of a speeding yacht.

A young woman on staff approaches and asks if she can help me. I let her know I'm waiting for the others to come to their senses. She smiles and moves on. This is the sort of exchange I can handle. She's an employee. I am a client. The rules of engagement are clear.

But if I tried to speak with her as an ordinary

man interested in an ordinary woman — it wouldn't happen. I'd freeze up like iced cod.

When they leave the platform, I quickly feign great interest in a nearby kayak, running a hand along the smooth surface.

John stops. "You want to take that out, I am totally down for it. There has to be some rapids somewhere."

I realize the kayak seats two. "I will let you know should an opportunity arise," I say.

"Sweet," he says and turns to their little party. "Come on. Let's go to the top of the ship and see if there's a diving spot."

"You are so crazy," the girl says with a laugh.

"Hey," Brady says. "You should come hang with us. We'll try not to get thrown off the ship."

I hesitate. There is no harm in tagging along with them for an afternoon. Perhaps there is something I could learn from their easy camaraderie.

Plus I can invite the businessman to Monte Carlo.

I follow them up. The bull rider once again extolls the virtues of riding a wild animal for eight seconds before leaping off or getting thrown.

The girl hangs on his arm. "I don't think I can even watch now," she says. "If you get tossed off that snorting hamburger, I'll have to grill it myself."

Curious. She seems to have a concern for his welfare already. Perhaps there is more to their exchange than loose sex.

My presence seems to keep them acting properly for most of the afternoon. We sit up top of the boat, watching other vessels go by, ordering lunch and drinking at the bar. One of the couples I invited joins us, and I become more in my element, chatting them up, finding just the right compliment to stoke their egos. They plan a venture with other friends to stay in the hotel adjoined to my casino, and I assure them I will get them into the exclusive class.

If only I could woo a date as well as I charm clients.

Mitch sits with us while the other two brutes pretend they are going to throw the girl overboard. After the other couple leaves, he asks, "You here on business too?"

"Mixing business and pleasure," I say.

The girl shouts and laughs, drawing our attention to them again.

"The young woman is quite vivacious," I say.

"She lives up to her name."

"What was it again?"

"Vivienne."

"Yes." I sip my scotch. The bull rider is kissing her now. It's quite passionate. So I was right about them sharing her.

"This seems like an unusual arrangement," I say.

Mitch clears his throat. "It is. Not one I ever pictured."

"Well, if you would like to show her a good time on your own, I would love to see the two of you in Monte Carlo. Have you ever been?"

Mitch takes a handful of cashews from a dish and pops them in his mouth. He shakes his head. "Can't say I have."

"It's an ideal place for both relaxation and for business. Surely you are aware of the tax benefits."

He looks me straight in the eyes now. "I'm aware. I haven't moved any assets there. Are you saying I should reconsider?"

"Yes, and perhaps establish a residency. Lots of benefits to that as well."

He nods.

Now the senator's son is behind the girl, wrapping his arms around her waist, his hands roaming to her breasts. My throat tightens a little, and I look away.

"Have your secretary contact our facility," I say. "I'd be more than happy to give you a personal tour and arrange some introductions."

I'm not sure he's listening now, watching both the men kiss and fondle the girl. He might be jealous. I'm not sure.

They wander over to us, arm in arm.

"You two going to hang up here for a while?" John asks. "We might make use of the room."

I'll have to have the bedding changed.

Or not. Last night I caught whiff of the girl, a light floral scent that was quite pleasing on my pillow.

Still, the men.

"I'll be down in a bit," Mitch says.

The others head toward the interior of the vessel.

"What happens at the cruise end?" I ask.

"John heads to his new SEAL team," Mitch says. "Brady will be back on the rodeo circuit."

"And you?"

"I'll be in Miami."

"With Vivienne."

He doesn't answer, just takes another handful of nuts.

If he's anxious to go down and join the others, he doesn't show it. I like this about him. It's probably why he does so well in business. You don't know what he's thinking.

The bell rings, signaling the dinner hour.

"Would you like to dine together?" I ask him.

He hesitates, then gestures to his swim trunks. "I'm not dressed for it. We've been eating in the room. You could join us there, of course."

I try to picture the debauchery going on and can't imagine. "Another time, perhaps."

He stands and shakes my hand. But as he heads down to the stateroom and I go to the dining lounge, my thoughts are definitely with the girl, picturing myself in their stead.

With Vivienne.

32: Brady the Bull Rider

This is without a doubt the best hundred thou I will ever spend.

Vivienne is amazing. She'll do anything, always eager, always fun.

I'm totally falling in love with this woman.

The shower was too small for all three of us, so John stepped aside and I'm in there with her. The suds are making her slippery, and I cannot for the life of me keep my hands off her.

Not that she'd want me to let go. She's giggling and sliding herself up and down me.

This is entirely too good to be true.

"Sit down," she orders, and I'm there.

She stands over me, and I lift my face to those glorious thighs, spreading just for me. I see where she wants my mouth. I love every sound she makes, every cry, every laugh. When she starts getting intense, holding on to the rail, her response to me is like cocaine.

I get her off twice before we finally turn off the water and I release her to John. By then Mitch is there too, and she's happy as a lark to fall onto the bed with both of them. I offer to order food and booze and set to that task while they have their fun.

This is the craziest thing. I couldn't imagine loving it. But I am.

We're halfway through eating when the door opens and Adolfo comes in.

Thankfully, everyone's semi-dressed, and we're acting more or less like normal people having dinner.

Adolfo pauses. "I was just coming to switch into a sports coat," he says.

"How was the dining room?" I ask. "I guess we'll get there one night."

"All very well." He heads to the closet in the hall.

"We're thinking of heading to the piano bar later," I tell him. I'm anxious to spend more time with him. While I was fooling around with Vivienne up top, Mitch got to talk to him privately. I need to do that too. My life savings is counting on it.

"You haven't lived until you've heard Vivienne

sing," John says.

"Really?" Mitch exclaims. "You've heard her?"

"You haven't?" I ask. "We went to a karaoke bar the night we met! She knocked everybody dead."

"You took that deadbeat to a karaoke bar?" John asks.

"I sang for you," she says with a laugh. "Don't get jealous at this late date."

"Well I haven't heard her," Mitch says. "I know your aspirations are to be a country music singer."

"They are," she says. "And tonight is called practice. Let's blow this hot dog stand. I believe there is a red evening gown calling my name."

She heads to the hall, where Adolfo has pulled out a light brown jacket. As he slides it on, she pulls out the red dress.

"We'll help you put it on," John says. "Get over here."

"No way," she says. "I want to make an entrance." She disappears into the bathroom.

Adolfo starts to head out, but I hold out my arm to stop him.

"You don't want to miss this," I tell him. "We'll get her to sing us a song before we go."

He glances across the room, and I can see he doesn't understand what's going on here. I guess it makes sense. It's more than a little unorthodox.

"Are you taking advantage of that poor girl?" he asks.

That makes John jump right off the sofa. "You say one more thing about Vivienne and I'll kill you," he says.

Adolfo takes a step back. I leap to my feet to get between them.

"Hey, hey," I say. "He's just worried about Viv. You wouldn't want anyone messing with her either, would you?"

John drops his fists. I certainly wouldn't want to be on his bad side.

"If you say she is okay with this arrangement, I will believe you," Adolfo says, his eyes flickering over to Mitch for a moment. "I just wouldn't want to see her come to any harm."

"No way," John says. "She's the best thing to happen to any of us."

My gut twists that the situation might be wrecking my chances to get that endorsement with Adolfo. He doesn't approve of what we're doing.

But I'm not about to let Viv go either.

"You should drop by the piano bar," I say. "Hear her sing."

Adolfo gives me a tight nod and opens the door.

As soon as it closes, John says, "Fucker."

"He's the voice of the world," Mitch says. "Remember that we're outside of reality at the moment. Not everyone will approve."

"Then they can suck my dick," John says. "And I'll jizz down their throats."

Mitch shakes his head. "Not everything is settled with threats and insults."

I wonder if they're going to come to blows too when the bathroom door opens.

And nobody thinks about anything but Vivienne.

She's pinned her hair up, little curls spilling out. She's added some makeup around her eyes, and she looks like a movie star. The dress molds her body, pushing her boobs into the most magnificent cleavage ever seen on a woman.

"Shit, Viv, we're not going to make it an hour before we want that dress off you," I say.

"You boys are going to have to keep your dicks to yourselves for a few hours." She strikes a dramatic pose, chin high, hand on her hip. "I'm going to *sing.*"

The rest of us rush to put on pants and nice shirts.

"Adolfo wore a sport coat," I say. "Do we need one?" I only own one suit jacket to my name, and it probably wouldn't pass with this fancy crowd.

"Not necessary," Mitch says. "Not for the lounge."

If the rich guy isn't going to wear one, I won't either. But Vivienne definitely outclasses us all as we head down the hall and up the stairs.

Only a smattering of guests are hanging out on this level. A man plays the piano, something classical. Across the room, the door to the casino is open and I spot a couple playing blackjack. Adolfo crosses the entrance. Figures he'd hang out in there. I'll go find him after Viv plays a few numbers. I don't have a dollar to my name for betting, but I can hang out and watch the other players.

Viv approaches the musician. Her red dress fits right in with his tuxedo and the glossy shine of the grand piano. She was meant for this.

Mitch, John, and I sit at a table nearby. A woman approaches and asks if we would all like our usual. Crazy how they keep track.

Mitch accepts for all of us and we keep our eye on Vivienne. She leans down and talks quietly with the man. He keeps playing, nodding and listening.

He transitions into a new song, and Vivienne hums along, then makes a little gesture to drop it down. The song stays the same, but he plays it differently, lower notes.

There's no microphone, but she's the kind of singer who can belt it out.

I'm not sure of the song at first, but several people in the room clap at the opening words. I kick back and sip the drink that has just arrived — damn, they have good liquor here. And I think, this is the life. The booze. The girl. The amazing surroundings. A day on the sea. Friends. I laugh a little inside. Crazy connection between us, all being so hot for Vivienne. But it's working.

Probably we won't get the whole ten days without someone clocking someone's jaw, but ain't nobody gonna say we're not livin' it up.

She comes around to the chorus and now I know the song. She belts out the title line and points to all of us.

"I'm saving all my love for you!"

John gets this big-ass grin and Mitch nods with a smile.

I had no idea this would ever work.

I glance back at the casino door, and Adolfo is standing there, drink in hand, watching Vivienne with full attention. I chuckle to myself. Probably every man in here has their eyes on her.

The glitter to her dress flashes bits of light as she moves. This is a Whitney song, but Viv's got her own spin on it. She's knocking everybody dead.

She makes eye contact with me, and it brings me back to the night we met. She's no ordinary girl, and I sure hope she makes it in this business. I remember the video she asked me to send out. I'll have to ask her if I helped. She's more than overdue for a big break.

Adolfo has come out now and sits at a table near the back. He watches with intensity, and this gives me an idea. Those fancy casinos have singing acts. Why doesn't he hire Viv? She's way more likely to get discovered in a place like that than in some video on YouTube.

And that's when I realize — what happens to me doesn't matter. I can ride bulls, keep my career going. I'm already the top of my field.

But Viv deserves this shot.

And I make it my mission to get Adolfo to hire her.

33: Vivienne

The next day we dock in Cuba.

The three boys have different excursions booked. That was my original plan when my intention was to keep them apart.

John is supposed to parasail. Mitch is scheduled to tour a fort and a basilica. But everyone agrees to go snorkeling on Brady's schedule instead.

John and Brady convince me to wear the micro bikini, which I agree only if one of them goes and finds a cute cover-up and some decent walking sandals.

John returns from the boutique with a pretty emerald green wrap that twists around my neck and falls in loose folds. The white sandals are sturdy and well padded. I don't recognize the brand, but I'm sure when I look them up, I'll want to die that I own them.

We walk the gangplank and are greeted by residents as we head to the meeting place for the snorkeling excursion. An old woman is selling necklaces interlaced with shells and beads. I look at one only for a moment before Mitch hands her money and fastens it around my neck.

I touch it for a moment. "Thank you," I tell him.

We pass a rack of hats and John plucks one off. "This is Vivienne all the way," he says. It's bright yellow with a green ribbon that matches my wrap.

I put it on and strike a pose, chin high.

"Love it," John says. And it's mine too.

"Come on," I say, "we're going to miss the ride."

We're loaded onto an open-topped bus with a few other people from the tour, including Adolfo and another couple.

"Snorkeling today?" he asks us.

"I love snorkeling," I tell him. "Especially in salt water. It's easy to float and there are so many things to see."

"You do this often then?" he asks.

"I take a fair amount of cruises," I say. "I'm a travel agent. Or was." God, I can't even imagine what horror is waiting for me when I get home. Fired, probably. Hopefully they don't withhold the commissions. Can they do that? They clients are all here. They all paid.

They're all happy.

The agency better not stiff me. I'll be screwed.

John places his hand on my thigh, and Adolfo's eyes gravitate to that touch, then back up to my face. I'm being judged. It's easy to feel happy with my situation when nobody's looking. I squirm a little.

The other couple is oblivious, though, and we chat about other places they've been and I've been. The bus doesn't drive far before we arrive at the dock where we get on a small boat that will take us out to the reef.

The wind on my face as we motor out into the wide blue sea is salty and warm. I close my eyes, reveling in the moment. It's stolen time, and I can't think ahead to what lies at the end. Just enjoy this.

The boat slows and anchors. The man running the tour explains about the fish and the reef and not to touch or stand on it. He passes out fins and masks, and the others prepare to go in.

I kick off my sandals and untie the wrap, aware of the men watching me. I fiddle with the little bits of the suit, feeling self conscious.

John stands close, his hand protectively on my waist. We get a little surprise when the woman in the other couple goes topless. I forget that in other countries, that's all expected and normal.

"See," John whispers. "You're fine."

She and her husband jump in first. I turn to pick up my mask and see Adolfo watching me. His eyes touch me everywhere, then come to meet my gaze.

Mitch told me Adolfo said he was worried the others were taking advantage of me, which made me laugh. But I see that he is paying attention. I pick up my mask and turn away.

The views are breathtaking. The pink reef, tangled and vast. Schools of fish, brightly colored, striped, patterned. We spot a small barracuda from the distance, silvery and sleek.

I swim with all three of them, their powerful strong bodies sometimes carrying me with them. John is particularly agile in the water. He dives down and swims below me on his back, allowing our bodies to brush together.

My emotions spill over, surrounded by such beauty and care and companionship. I want to live every moment and hold it tight.

One of the tour guides swims up with his underwater camera. John, Brady, and I get silly under the water, striking goofy poses. Then Mitch comes near, taking me from the others. He turns us in the water, straight up and down, like an undersea dance. My hair spins out and I'm like a mermaid to his sailor.

The three men agree to a race to one of the reefs, and I bow out, slowly heading back toward the boat. I see a lone figure drifting along and realize it's Adolfo.

I hope I can take this chance to apologize for inconveniencing him, so I move his direction. He's watching a sea turtle swim toward the surface.

I brush against him as I approach, and he turns. We can't speak with the masks, but he points out a group of very tiny bright red fish. They swim fervently one direction, then abruptly turn, all at the exact same moment, and go the other way.

I wonder how they know to do it, if the leader has some signal, or if they all respond to the precise same instinct.

Adolfo and I look at each other and smile around our mouthpieces. He kicks himself vertical, and I follow suit. We break the surface and push our masks up on our heads.

"That was amazing!" I say. "They are so in sync!"

"Quite beautiful," he says. "Are you having a good time?"

"The best," I say.

"I see you've lost your entourage."

I glance back over to the reef. The others have

just come up, slapping Mitch on the back. He seems to have surprised them all by winning the race.

"They're more athletic than I am."

"How about we couch potatoes head back to the boat?"

We pull ourselves up the ladder and return the mask and fins to the tour.

The other couple are already back as well, sitting together near the front of the boat, the woman snuggled into the man. He is massaging her bare breasts as they kiss.

Adolfo and I turn away at the same time. I guess anything really goes on these cruises.

We sit with our backs to them.

"Are you from Miami?" Adolfo asks.

"No, Tennessee, actually," I say.

"Why the move?"

"I wanted to escape my parents. I had a boyfriend at the time who moved to Miami. He didn't last, but my love for the city did. There's just so much to do."

His gaze rakes my body for a second, and I wonder if I can gracefully go fetch my cover-up.

"I heard you sing last night," he says. "You were quite good. I think the whole boat ended up listening."

My cheeks warm up. "It was fun. I think we're doing it again tonight."

"I shall look forward to that."

I pause, trying to find the words to say to him about my screwup.

"Listen, Mr. Felini —"

"Adolfo, please,"

"Adolfo. I'm very sorry I messed up your room. Blue Sapphire said they were holding rooms, and I needed three. And you had three. And I could edit it, which I thought meant it was saved for me."

"Do not worry about it," he says. "It has worked out. Are the deck beds all right?"

I flash to the two rather torrid nights under the stars, sleeping with one or sometimes two of the guys. There were four beds on each side of a high wall, and we had all four on our side. Thankfully. "They are great. I don't mind at all."

"If you decide you need a night indoors, I am happy to switch with you," he says.

"That's very sweet of you," I say.

The driver calls out. It's time to head back.

The boys swim in, and I stop to admire the sure strokes of their arms, the water streaming across their strong backs. I see why Mitch won. He might not have the pure power of the other two, but he's leaner in the water, with no wasted movement.

They jump up, dripping, onto the back of the boat, and I excuse myself from Adolfo to help them dry off and put away their masks.

As we return to shore, the tour guide serves us fish cooked in foil with strange vegetables and dark spices. On the ride to the dock, we jump off the bus early and wander the market, picking up bits of food and thick drinks. I buy a silver bracelet for Sam.

Mitch spots a lovely length of silky pink cloth embroidered in gold. "Do you like it?" he asks.

"It's lovely," I say.

And then it's mine, wrapped around my shoulders. I need a bag to carry everything, and John plucks a simple straw one from an elderly woman's cart, paying her double what she asks.

We head back to the port to dress for dinner. I tie the pink fabric into a Sari-like wrap. We sit together at a table in the main dining hall, flickering candles and fresh flowers at every table.

It's been a lovely, glorious day.

If only it could last.

34: Adolfo from Monte Carlo

I confess that I have also become smitten with the girl.

Part of it is her easy joy with those men. Every time I encounter them the next day on the streets of Cienfeugos, they are laughing, eating, feeding each other, kissing. I wonder how this strange quartet came to be.

I am jealous.

The other part of my infatuation is the soul with which she sings. I could not stay away last night and sat alone at a table, marveling at her voice and the emotion she brought to every song.

Our brief time in the water and on the boat is often on my mind. I spoke to her then, and I did not freeze up. My anxiety was manageable. This is rare and should be considered carefully. Why is she different?

All day as I walk with another couple, I watch for glimpses of her in the shops and restaurants. I purchase a ring, silver inlaid with gemstones, with her in mind. I want to give her something, to have an excuse to talk to her again. I rehearse how I might explain the gift. Her singing, perhaps.

I pray for rain. Rain on the ocean that would drive her inside to our stateroom. I would lock the others out and keep her for myself.

The thought of kissing her and holding that body close to mine becomes a fantasy.

That night she sings again. Her men sit close as I turn the slender ring over and overin my coat pocket. She has a new dress, no doubt from the market today, pale blue like the ocean that surrounds us. It flows down her body like a waterfall.

When she sings about finding a one true love, I cannot take the excruciating pain of having her sing to the other three. I head back into the casino, finding my rhythm, teaching passengers how to maximize their bets and inviting them to my property in Monte Carlo.

When the clapping ends and the singing is over, I excuse myself.

I will find her, give her the gift. Take the moments I can with her.

They are easy to spot, raucous and happy, sitting at one of the lounge bars near the piano. I approach and they elbow each other.

Brady, the bull rider who always wants my attention, says, "Pull up a stool!"

"Thank you," I say, but don't choose one. Instead, I walk directly up to her. "Your singing was divine, as always."

She turns to me. "Thank you, Adolfo."

I see in her eyes the relief that I have not held a grudge against her. "Might I make a request for tomorrow night?"

The other men get quiet, watching me with suspect eyes. They think I mean to steal her away. It must be my tone. My anxiety rises, but the rigid coldness that always renders me speechless with discomfort does not come.

Maybe the quack psychologist was correct. The one true love.

"Of course," she says. "Hopefully I will know it."

"It isn't a song," I say. I pull the ring from my pocket. "I found this in the market today and thought of you and your jewel-like voice. My request is that you wear it tomorrow when you sing."

I place it in her palm. She holds it up. "Adolfo, it's beautiful."

The other men shift on their stools. Now it is them who feel the discomfort.

"If it does not fit, I have been told there is a man on staff who can adjust it."

She slips it on a few different fingers, settling on the center of her left hand.

"It's perfect. Thank you." She looks up at me, her eyes bright, her hair a halo of red-gold. Then she slides off the stool and wraps her arms around me.

The feel of her body steals my breath. I place my hands on her back and hold on, lost in the light floral scent of her hair, the pressure of her breasts folding against my chest.

Someone clears their throat.

"Oh, hush," Vivienne says. "Or you can sleep in your own bed tonight."

She lets me hold her a moment longer, then pulls away. She lifts her hand to the light. "I will pick out a special song just for you tomorrow."

I give her a small bow. "I will await it most anxiously."

I'm about to step away when the strict woman from our first day walks up to the bar. She wears a stiff blue uniform, and her hair is the same tall gray beehive that I remember from the stateroom confrontation over the booking error.

Hilda, I believe.

She sees Vivienne, looks away, then snaps her head back. "What in the world?" she exclaims. "What are you doing on board this vessel?"

Vivienne's eyebrows shoot to her hairline and her expression crosses with fear. She backs into Brady, who puts his arms around her protectively.

"Back off," he says. "She's our guest."

"You haven't paid for a guest," Hilda says. "You chose the most minimum package available."

"I'll cover her," Mitch says. "I'll have the money wired in ten minutes."

"You don't even have a proper room," Hilda snaps. She grabs Vivienne's arm. "You're coming with me and we'll have you off the ship first thing in the morning when we come to port."

"That isn't necessary," Mitch says. "And you are being unreasonable."

"Am I?" Hilda asks. "I've heard about a trampy girl gallivanting all over this ship with inappropriate behavior and disrupting the music schedule in the lounge. I should have known it was her." She stares Vivienne in the face. "Obviously the mistake was a ruse to have these men sneak you on. You would never have qualified yourself."

"Hey now," Brady says. "There is no reason to treat her like this."

Hilda turns and takes several more steps away, dragging Vivienne with her.

John cuts her off, his body an immobile mass. "You will leave her with us. Or my father will hear about it."

"Please," Hilda says. "You are a grown man. Your father will not tolerate you doing anything that might harm his public image. And this girl will do just that."

She takes another step.

All three of them block her way.

"You're not taking her," Mitch says.

Hilda gives a false smile, then presses a button on the side of her Bluetooth ear piece. "Security to the lounge. We have a situation."

"Boys, please, don't," Vivienne says. "I'm not supposed to be here. I can't wreck your cruise."

She looks at Brady. "You need to keep talking to Adolfo." She turns to me. "You really want to sponsor him. He's better than any race car."

Before I can respond, she shifts her attention to John. "I have so many great excursions lined up for you. I couldn't do half of them anyway. Enjoy the danger."

And to Mitch. "I'm sure John is more than happy to help out with whatever you and his dad cooked up. I bet you two can work something out. You're both great schemers."

Two large men approach. I recognize their stance and look. I use the same company for my most important security detail in the high-stakes private rooms. They are known internationally for their exceptional training program. Even the Navy SEAL would have trouble taking on one of them, much less two.

"Take her to the office," Hilda says to them. "She can sleep on a cot in there until morning."

Everyone starts arguing with her at once as the men lead Vivienne away. I let them have their fit and back away to make a communication of my own. All three of them are new to Blue Sapphire, but I am not.

And neither is a particular one of my associates.

35: Vivienne

I had it coming.

I should have known I had no business being on the cruise.

This is my punishment for stealing more than my share of happiness.

Three men. And Adolfo, giving me that ring!

I stare at it as I sit in a chair in the corner of an office that looks nothing like the rest of the ship.

It's all gray walls and metal filing cabinets. One of the security men sits in a chair by the door, like I'm a common criminal. Maybe stealing my way onto a hundred-thousand-dollar cruise *is* a bit of a heist.

I finger the smooth satin fabric of the blue dress Mitch bought me. I wish I had the necklace on. It hadn't matched the outfit, so I left it behind. Surely they'll let me get my things. The clothes. Sam's bracelet. I'll need my purse and identification to get home.

If I can afford to get home. We're off the shore of Cuba!

But tomorrow is Grand Cayman. That's where they'll put me off. That's easy. I can fly home for a couple hundred dollars. This whole thing will end.

Tears start to slip down my cheeks. I knew the cruise would be over eventually, but we still had so much time!

I ache with the loss of those few days of bliss I would never get now.

Time to get back to reality.

The reality of no job.

Of making the agency lose the contract with Blue Sapphire.

Case in point eleven: I mess everything up. Especially anything good.

Gramma always told me to look for a silver lining in every cloud. And I'm searching. I have some memories, that's for sure.

Maybe it's time to pack up and move to Nashville. I won't have a good reference for my last job after this mess, but maybe Sam can fake it for me. I could get on with an agency there and really hit the auditions hard.

They liked me here on the ship. Even better than at FreakEasy. And the sets with Adrianna at John's hotel. Those were amazing.

I can do this. I just have to believe I can.

The door opens and I sit up straight, but it's just a crew member bringing a cot for me to sleep on. He sets it up somewhat apologetically.

"Thank you," I say.

"You're welcome."

"Hey."

He turns back. "Yes?"

"Can you send a message to Stateroom 307?"

The man glances nervously at the security guard. "What's that?"

"Just that I'm sorry. And thank you. And it was wonderful."

He nods. "Okay."

"Thank you."

When he's gone, I lie down on the cot. I'm suddenly crazy tired. All the late nights, the excursions, the swimming and walking and sun. It's been a lot. The best. But more than I'm used to.

Way more.

Despite my over-the-top ungodly behavior, I feel the hand of my mother on my forehead. And

Gramma behind her, steaming up some hot tea.

It was a wild time. I loved every minute.

But now it's over.

ॐ৪ৎ

I snap awake when the door opens. I can't tell if I've been asleep for a few minutes or all night. There's no porthole in this room, so I can't see the sun.

It's Hilda all right. I would know that beehive silhouette anywhere.

"Come along," she says.

Great. I'm literally about to walk the plank.

I stand up, my neck and back in knots from my sleeping arrangement. I pass the security guard. His eyes don't move as I follow Hilda out.

We head to the staircase.

"Have we docked?" I ask. It feels like the ship is still rolling.

"No," Hilda says sharply.

"Where am I going then?" I flash with the image of me actually walking off a long wood beam, arms tied behind my back.

"I've been overruled," she says. "I'm to return you to your stateroom."

"Really?" I wonder who it was. Mitch? Did he

buy her out? John? Did his father make a fuss after all?

But when we arrive at the open door of our room, only one person is inside.

Adolfo.

"Have a nice cruise," Hilda says stiffly and walks away.

I'm so relieved, I walk right up to him and give him a giant hug. He holds me tight, just like he did in the lounge when he gave me the ring.

"Are you all right?" he asks. "Nobody hurt you?"

"I'm fine," I say. "Where are the others?"

"At the bar."

"What time is it? How long have I been gone?"

"About four hours," he says. "It took a while for me to get in touch with the appropriate people."

"*You* did it?" I ask. I sink onto the sofa. "But I'm the one who screwed up your whole trip!"

Then I remember the ring.

"No, you actually saved it," he says. "May I?" he asks, gesturing to the cushion beside me.

"Of course," I say.

"You may know by now that I run one of the royal casinos in Monte Carlo," he says.

"Are you a prince?" I ask.

He laughs. "Oh no. I am just the manager. But it

is a very esteemed position. So I have a fair amount of pull."

"Oh God, did you sic a royal on Broom Hilda?" I ask.

Adolfo laughs, and for the first time, I see the amusement reach his eyes. "Vivienne, you are a treasure."

"Well, did you?"

"In a manner of speaking, yes. The Prince himself would not make this call, but his office. She will be defending her position to the owners of this cruise line when we return to Miami."

I hug him again. "Thank you, thank you, thank you."

His arms come around me, and I sense this time how he's holding on. How he's reveling in my closeness.

I let the embrace go on a little while, giving him this moment. Then I pull away.

"I really should see after the others. I'm sure they're worried."

"Yes, they are pulling all the strings they have," he says. "Mine are just faster."

I stand up. "I'm very much indebted to you. I'll dedicate every one of my songs to you."

"That isn't necessary. But if you should find

yourself…free." He hesitates, trying to form his words. "I would like very much for you to visit me in Monte Carlo. I would have everything arranged."

Oh. Wow.

"That's very generous."

"And even if you should not like to be my private guest," he goes on, and I can tell these words are harder for him. "I would very much like to explore the possibility of you singing in one of our lounges. Our large acts are booked two years out, but we have many cabarets, and I could move you up over time, I am sure."

"You're handing me the world," I say.

"You deserve the world," he says simply. "You have something few people possess. Life. Passion. You are bold."

I'm speechless. "Thank you, Adolfo." I look around and spot a Blue Sapphire notepad. I scribble my cell phone down. "So you can find me."

"Thank you," he says, and tucks the paper into his pocket.

I hurry out the door then. There are seventeen million bars on this boat, but I figure I know where they are.

And sure enough, they're poolside, surrounded by empty bottles. The place is deserted, the night sky inky black and full of stars.

John sees me first. "Oh my God, Vivienne!" He leaps from the stool and runs across the deck, lifting me up against him and swinging me around. "You're all right!"

"Of course I am, silly," I say, smacking him on the back. "They weren't going to bind and torture me."

"We were so worried they would turn you in to authorities," Brady says. "We pictured you in some Cuban jail, getting sold into the sex trade."

"The next port of call is Grand Cayman," I say. "They're perfectly civilized."

John doesn't want to let me go, but I fight my way down to hug Mitch and Brady.

"I slept on a cot, then Hilda came and sprung me."

"What made her change her mind?" Mitch asks. "I put in a dozen phone calls to no avail."

"Yeah, my own dad didn't take my call on this one," John says.

"Adolfo," I say. "He knew people that made Hilda back off."

"Good ol' Adolfo," Brady says. "We should take him some booze."

I look around at all the bottles. The bar is

shuttered. "Did you raid the liquor cabinet or something?"

"Naw, the bartender felt sorry for us and left us some things to tide us over until morning," Brady says.

Mitch slaps John on the back. "We even got John here to get drunk."

"It was the proper occasion," he says.

"Well, I'm here, and I'm exhausted," I say.

"Should we go change in the stateroom?" Mitch asks.

"I don't want to bother Adolfo again," I say. I remember how he spoke to me, the longing in his voice. It might be hard for him to see me with these boys so soon.

"Naked it is!" John says, and sweeps me off my feet.

He carries me up to Deck 6 and our beds. They wrestle with the foundations for a moment and finally manage to push them all together, creating one huge surface.

We slide out of our clothes and leave them in a big pile. I'm grateful for our side of the wall as the boys show me how worried they were. How lost.

The sun is rising by the time we finally go to sleep.

36: Mitch the Billionaire

I could not be more relieved that Vivienne was returned to us.

I only wish I had been the one to save her.

Grand Cayman is an overnight stop, so none of us are too anxious to get up and around too early. The ship can't dock here but has to be tendered out at sea. Guests take small motor boats to the shore.

We watch from the empty top deck, sipping mimosas and wrapped in blankets. I realize how far I've come from my perfect suits and proper behavior. I've spent the night with a woman and two other men in the open air of a cruise ship, haven't bothered to shave in two days, and now I'm curled up naked with Vivienne inside a bedsheet.

The small boat down below loads up, goes to

shore, and motors back.

John starts doing pushups and all manner of calisthenics without a stitch on. A young woman comes up with breakfast and almost drops her tray when she sees him.

"Don't scare everyone," Vivienne says.

"Uh, I don't mind," the girl says, setting the dishes down and backing away slowly.

Brady shakes his head. He's put his boxers on at least.

"We're going feral," I say.

John thumps his fists on his chest and lets out caveman cry.

A couple of the staff on the ramp down below look up.

"We're going to get thrown off the boat before this is over," I tell him.

"Not me," Vivienne says. "I've got royalty on my side."

"Come here, you haughty wench," John shouts and throws aside the sheet to snatch her from me. He picks her up and carries her over to the other side of the wall where our beds are.

The ones on this side remain empty. Apparently we've scared off all the other guests who tried them, or else the novelty wore off. We've had Deck 6 to ourselves.

Giggles and happy cries come from the other side of the wall, and Brady and I shake our heads at each other. Last night while Vivienne was gone, we talked about what was best for her and if we should back off.

We didn't come to any conclusions, although both Brady and John said they'd be traveling once the cruise was over. John to his new SEAL assignment. Brady back on the rodeo circuit.

Which leaves me in Miami with Vivienne.

I've taken a step back, knowing that I have the best shot at a real relationship with her. When it comes to the long game, I'm a master.

They return after a while, Vivienne all rosy on her cheeks and thighs. She holds a sheet and works to wrap it around her.

"We should head to the stateroom for clothes," I say. "What's the excursion today?"

"Oh, it's the bioluminescence cave for John," Vivienne says. "I booked a private one for him away from the tourists. It will be amazing."

"Can we come?" Brady asks. "Or is this a solo deal?"

"We can call the guide," Vivienne says.

"I have a signal here," I say. "You have their number?"

"In my phone," she says. "In the room." She tilts her head. "I know the ports of call, but I've lost all track of dates. Is it February yet?"

"The second," I tell her.

Her eyes get wide. "Oh my gosh! Oh my gosh!"

"What is it?" Brady asks.

"The audition with Gold Discography Records!" she says. "The one you helped me get views for! They picked last night!"

"Where can you find out?" Brady asks.

"On my phone!" Vivienne says. "Except I don't have an international plan. I can't check my email!"

I hand her my phone. "Can you use mine?"

She takes it. "I can go to the forums. Or the site. They should have announced who got in."

We sit at a table near the rail, the food forgotten. Vivienne keys in letters, and the rest of us wait.

John pours a round of mimosas.

"I found the list," Vivienne says finally. "I'm afraid to look."

Brady takes the phone. "I'll look. John, get this girl some food."

I help unload the dishes and butter a piece of toast for Vivienne.

Brady starts reading. "Gold Discography Records is pleased to be auditioning the following applicants at our studio in Nashville, Tennessee in three weeks."

"That's good," John says. "You'll have time to get back and get there."

"If I'm in," Vivienne says. I press a piece of toast to her lips to silence her negativity. She takes a bite.

Brady goes on. "Auditions do not mean a contract will be offered. Yada yada."

"Just get on with the list!" John says. He stabs a bit of egg and eats it, then gives one to Vivienne.

"Looking," Brady says.

"Say them all," Vivienne says. "I want to know if any of my friends got in."

"Okay. Paul Johnson. Marie Simpson. José Rodriquez. Janie Summers."

"Janie!" Vivienne says. "Yay! She's so good!"

"Abdul Abboud. Dante Brown. Angelica Jiminez." He stops.

"Keep going, bro," John says. "We want to hear the whole list."

Brady still says nothing.

"Did you lose the signal?" I ask.

Brady sighs and passes me the phone. "That was the whole list."

"What? No way." I take the phone and scroll through it.

But he's right.

"Assholes!" John says, slamming his fist on the table. "They don't know shit!"

Vivienne looks out over the water.

"It was probably some crap contract anyway," Brady says. "They stick it to newbies who don't know what they're signing."

"I wouldn't let her sign anything to her disadvantage," I say.

Brady elbows me. "You're rich. Just buy the damn company and make them sign her."

"No," Vivienne says. "Nobody's going to buy my way in. That's not how I want to do it."

I could have told them that.

"Trust me, people are bought and sold every day," John says.

"Not me," she insists. "It's one thing to fail on your own terms. It's another to buy your way in and still have them hate you."

"Nobody's going to hate you," Brady says. "I've seen you sing two different places. Everybody loves you."

"I've seen it too," John says. "You're just getting a leg up to catch your break."

"Look at me," Vivienne says. She stands up and lets the sheet fall. She squeezes her thigh, her belly. "They wanted video links to see us, what we look like.

And I'm not star material."

"You happen to be pointing out all the things I love," John says.

"Me too," Brady says.

"Stop it!" she says. "You're only saying that because you're fucking me!"

That gets us quiet.

She starts crying then, and we take turns holding her. I figure she's seen her fair share of rejection as she followed this dream.

And Brady's right. I could front her first record. I could put a marketing team on her.

But she wants it her way. And I'm going to honor that.

37: Vivienne

Well, I'm the Debbie downer nobody needs right now.

Most of the cruise guests are on the island. I don't want to do anything, so I send John and Brady down to the bottom deck to try out the jet skis.

Mitch takes me to the stateroom for a shower and some TLC. He's sweet and caring and I'm happy to fall into him for the afternoon.

It gets time for the bioluminescence tour, and I call the guide to say we'll have extras. Mitch leaves to go fetch the others, and I'm alone for the first time in days.

I stand naked in front of the mirror, holding up the red micro bikini. I can't bear to put it on. It's just ridiculous. I'm ridiculous.

I'm nothing.

Damn this shame wave. I'm up to my ears in it with this rejection by the record label. The boys are the only reason I haven't gone under.

I toss the bikini aside and lift up the retro one piece. At least this one is cute on.

I should do my hair a little different for it. I set the suit on the counter and twist my hair up. I could really use my combs and some bobby pins, but I'll make do with the ponytail that was in my purse.

The door opens and I say, "About time you made it! We'll probably have to call someone to make sure we can get to shore."

I hear a sharp intake of breath and look in the mirror's reflection through the open door.

It's Adolfo.

"Oh!" I say and snatch up the suit to hold in front of me. It doesn't cover much. I have to choose between the boobs or the thatch.

"You are more beautiful than I imagined," he says, then turns away. "I'll leave you to your privacy."

He's more of a gentleman than those other hoodlums.

I shove my feet in the leg holes and yank the suit on. "I thought you would be on shore," I say.

"I had a conference call this morning," he says,

his back still turned. "I missed the proverbial boat."

"We're headed to the shore," I say, fixing my straps. "You can hop on ours."

He pulls a pair of swim trunks from a shelf. "It already seems that I am. Your, eh, suitors were quite pleased about my rescue of you from that horrid woman. They invited me along on your luminary cave swim."

"Bioluminescence," I say.

He begins to unbutton his shirt. I watch, curious about this man who has asked me to visit him in a place I've never been. Monte Carlo. I've booked a few trips for people there. It's expensive.

He tugs his shirt from his shoulders and drops it in the laundry bag the staff picks up each evening. His chest is smooth and solid. He's not tricked out like John or Brady, and maybe even a little leaner than Mitch. But firm and perfect just the same. He has a small patch of hair in the center, and I have a crazy urge to touch it.

He hesitates and I realize I'm hogging the bathroom.

"Oh!" I say and step out. "It's all yours."

He nods and we trade places.

I turn to the closet and look for my sundress to wear over the suit. "You been to Cayman before?" I ask.

He shuts the door only partway so we can still talk. I realize that if I stand by the mirrored panel on the closet, I can see an angled reflection of him in the bathroom mirror. He unbuckles his pants.

A girl should know what she's been invited to.

"I have," he says. "Stingray Island is quite a place."

"I've heard about it," I say, shifting so I can get a better look as he lowers his pants. He's a boxer guy. Satin. "You can pet them and some will even kiss you."

"I didn't go that far," he says.

Now the boxers drop.

And. Wow.

I stumble a little into the mirror and smack my nose. "Ow."

His head peeks out. "You okay?"

"Just my usual klutzy self." I turn to him. He isn't really hidden by the door. I get a full glimpse of his chest, belly, and there it is again. Whoa.

As I stare, it responds. He's a shower *and* a grower.

"My apologies," he says, backing away. "Let me get dressed."

Damn, I'm full of urges.

I want to touch that.

I want to do more with it.

But I do the right thing. I turn away and pull my dress off the hanger.

ca&so

The five of us squeeze onto a small rowboat with the guide, a lean, dark-skinned man in his twenties. We didn't have room to bring anything, so all our clothes, shoes, and phones are locked at the marina.

He takes us carefully through the water in the dark. All around are tourists waving their hands in the water to stir up the tiny glowing plankton.

It's pure magic, just as I remembered. I dip my fingers in the water, creating a glowing flow of blue light. It's like pixie dust.

"Beautiful," Adolfo says. He reaches out as well.

"There's three types of bioluminescent microorganisms here," the tour guide says. "They light up when you disturb the water, as a sort of defense mechanism against predators."

But we're not stopping here. Around the cove, according to our guide, is a small underwater cave that is just as bright. They don't ordinarily take tourists because to go, you have to dive under a rock wall and come up inside the enclosure.

But we're doing it.

I'm a little nervous. It's dark, and as we row away from the tourists, the water is quiet and still. It feels like you could fall out of this boat and disappear into nothingness.

John sits behind me and puts a hand on my bare shoulder. "This is gorgeous," he says. "Thank you for arranging it."

I lay my hand on top of his. "My pleasure."

We approach an outcropping of rock. The man drops a small anchor. "Here's where we get out. I'll lead the way. Follow my light."

He puts on a headlamp. With a little splash, he lands in the water.

John jumps in next and holds his hands out to me. "Brady, help her," he says.

Between the two of them, I manage to make it into the water beside them. "Easier getting out than going back in," I say.

"We'll help," John says.

Brady and Mitch hop out, followed by Adolfo. When we're all in the water, our guide motions us to follow.

Already there are pale trails of light that follow our paths. The guide takes us along the rock wall, then points down.

He dives and disappears.

"I'll go next," John says. "Then Vivienne."

He also disappears.

My heart hammers. I take a deep breath, then push myself down. At first I can't find the bottom of the wall, and I panic a little. Then I see the light and dive down farther.

John finds my hands and pulls me toward him. We rise to the surface together.

And I can't believe what I see.

Blue. Everywhere is blue.

The water glows with an ethereal light. The guide is a dark shadow, his small, round white lamp the only color other than unending blue.

Brady makes his way into the cave, then Mitch. Then Adolfo.

When everyone breaks the surface, we turn in circles, watching the light dance in our wake.

John splashes forward, leaving a bright blue trail.

"This is unbelievable," Mitch says.

The walls of the cave glow faintly.

"This is a rare thing to see," the guide says.

"I'll say," says Brady.

We are all awestruck. I find a rock and stand easily, head and shoulders above water, moving my arms like a butterfly. The water forms blue wings with my motion.

"I'm an angel," I say.

"That you are," Adolfo says.

Brady dives down, and I watch him make his way to me, blue trailing him like magic. He rises up and holds me tight, spinning us both now that he has his footing. "I'll never forget this," he says.

I won't either.

I break from Brady and swim in a lazy circle, watching the blue trail alight behind me. The men all stop, watching me.

"Now that's a vision," Adolfo says.

"It is," Mitch agrees.

I swim back to them. "Isn't it magical?" I ask.

"You're like a mermaid of light," Mitch says. He comes close, unable to take his eyes off me. He whispers in my ear, "So much better without the suit."

John hears him and turns to the guide. "Spot you two hundred dollars to wait in the boat."

"Works for me," he says. "I'll come back in half an hour."

"Make it an hour," Brady says. His eyes are on me too. And I know that look.

The guide dives beneath the wall with a splash. Without his light, the room is fully blue, all of us silhouettes in an otherworldly glow.

Mitch slides the strap of my suit off my shoulder. I let him, shivering as my senses overload. The beauty, the isolation, these men.

I remember that Adolfo is here. As Mitch peels the bathing suit off my body, another ripple of anticipation goes through me. Will he be a part of this? The others have been so protective.

It's my choice, I decide. These men don't own me.

I push off the floor and swim to Brady, tugging at his swim trunks. "Off," I say.

Then to John. "None of this," I say, pulling on the elastic of his Speedo.

I turn to Mitch. He spreads my suit on a high rock, out of the water. "You too."

Then I turn to Adolfo. "I would like very much for you to join us."

His eyes take in my body. That beautiful dick of his starts to move, filling out the pale green swim trunks. "Are you sure?" he asks.

I glide forward to him and take his hands. "I am," I say, pressing them to my breasts.

He touches me slowly, the tips of my nipples, the swells, then down to my waist, the flare of my hips. He pulls me to him, and our lips meet.

His kiss is soft, almost uncertain. I press against him, feeling him hard against me.

My fingers find the waistband of his trunks. I slide my hand inside, grasping the length of him.

He holds his breath, his mouth against mine.

I stroke him with one hand and pull the trunks down with the other. I toss them behind me and hear John say, "Got it." This makes me smile against his lips.

"Do they always work together like this?" he asks.

"Always," I say. "I have taught them to."

This gets a laugh from behind me.

"She's kinda right," Brady says.

"I don't know how to be," Adolfo whispers.

"I'll show you," I tell him.

"Just relax and enjoy it," John says. "You get into it."

By the throbbing in my hand, he already is.

John swims over and folds in behind me, hands covering my breasts.

"Mmmm," I tell him. "Make me ready for Adolfo."

The cock in my hand quivers with my words.

John slides his fingers inside me. "So warm," he says.

I kiss Adolfo again, stroking him gently. We bob in the water, the blue spreading as I bounce on the sandy bottom and back up.

"We're not making you step out on anybody, are we bro?" John asks. "If you've got a wife or something, we'll totally back away."

Adolfo shakes his head. "No one," he says. He looks in my eyes, then down at my body, incredulous, devouring.

"Touch me," I tell him. "I'm yours."

John backs away.

Adolfo's hands learn the curves and valleys of me. He's gentle, almost timid as his fingers trail along my skin.

I reach up and slick his hair away from his face. His eyes drift closed. I hold on to his shoulders and wrap my legs around his hips.

His cock is between us, hot and hard. It's so big. Scary big. I want it desperately. I slide up his body, then down, letting him bump against where I want him to go.

I lean next to his ear. "Are you okay without protection?"

He nods, his hands on my waist.

I grab tight and force myself down.

My voice cries out as he opens me wide. I'm

dizzy, heady with it. God. It's incredible.

Around us, the water swirls, sparkling with blue light.

John returns, then Brady, then Mitch. They hold me and help me fight the water, pushing us together, letting us get lost in the pleasure as they do the work.

I've never felt anything like Adolfo, spreading me open, bumping against my insides. I gasp for breath.

"Let us hear you come, baby," John says.

Adolfo's eyes meet mine. Water drips from his hair into the water, creating little blue pools of light.

If an orgasm could have a color, this one would be white and blue, both shocking hot and cool.

It flashes through me like the light that surrounds us, bright and luminous. I'm lit up from within. My voice echoes off the rock walls, filling our space with sound.

"That's it," John says. "Now unload in her."

Adolfo's hands squeeze me tightly. His eyes close, his face tense.

Then I feel it, the shudder, the warm rush. I laugh, a sparkling sound in the cave.

"Love it!" I tell him and kiss his cool mouth. "Please say we can do that again on the boat."

He opens his eyes. "I am in love with you," he says.

"Join the club, bro," John says.

I slide off Adolfo's body and float on my back. My breasts glow blue from the light. The air is warm, and the water is perfect. I kick around the cave as the men watch me.

John isn't shy about coming up to me next. He catches me and slides me on top of him, my back to his chest. His legs come around mine, and he's hard against me. "Let's push the envelope on positions, shall we?" he asks.

I laugh and reach up to hold his head as he reaches between us. It takes a few tries, but he manages to enter me from below.

We start to sink, so Brady helps out, keeping us afloat while John plunges in.

"Seems like something's missing," Mitch says and glides over to us to circle his thumb against my exposed clit, high above the water as John pushes me up.

The three of them work with me and I close my eyes, listening to the water lap against the cave walls, reveling in John's hard body below me, and Mitch's expert fingers working the nub.

A warm mouth closes over a breast and I open to see Adolfo there, full attention on my body.

Brady holds my hips steady as John moves more

aggressively. The feeling of being overwhelmed takes me over again. Mitch adds his mouth to his hands as my body bobs along the surface of the water. The orgasm starts from so many places, the warmth on my breast from Adolfo, the steady thick pressure from John, the practiced thrust of Mitch's tongue, and the safe security provided by Brady as we float along.

I cry out like I never have before. Tears add my salt to the sea. All around me is love and sex and passion and protection and care.

And light.

We glow.

38: Vivienne

So reader, you're still here.

It's okay if you judge.

I've been naughty.

Case in point twelve: I believe you only live once.

And I'm living four lives simultaneously.

I'm guessing you have questions.

I bet I know the big one.

How many dicks can fit in a girl at once?

We had five more nights to figure it out.

Spoiler alert: *all of them*.

Once we had the privacy of a stateroom, we looked it up on ye ol' porn site. Two could fit in the v-hole. One in the butt. And one in the mouth. We had pictures to go by. Mitch set up his laptop so we could see what parts went where.

I'm not going to say this was comfortable.

And the bed was part mattress, part Twister game board.

There were a lot of comments like, "John, move your damn knee." And "Mitch, get your fucking ass out of my face."

And a lot of laughs.

But we did it.

For maybe fifteen seconds.

Then we all fell in this crazy pile of limbs and skin and did stuff the old-fashioned way.

But all good things come to an end.

And so did the cruise.

No one was ready to part, so Mitch booked a super suite with four bedrooms at a Miami hotel. There, armed with cell signals and telephones and the real world, we put together what would happen next.

John called his dad, said Mitch Roberts was *the man* and that as soon as he finished his second contract with the SEALS, he was IN for the family politics.

Of course, that would be six years from now, and he'd figure out how to weasel out of it by then.

Mitch contacted a real estate agent in Monte Carlo and began a plan to establish a new office there as well as a residence. He would work with Adolfo to create a tax haven that would mean that even if John's dad screwed him over on the proposed legislation, he could still work out a business deal.

Mitch says this is called *hedging your bets*.

Adolfo says that is his favorite term.

It's like a bromance.

We all viewed footage of Brady riding a bull. I had to cover one eye, as it was hard to watch. Adolfo agreed to work out an endorsement deal and they sat together planning a strategy.

It was all working out.

Except for me.

I call Sam, and she says that due to some princess calling Lucky Vega, their Blue Sapphire status was restored and no one was mad.

However, in the days between when I left and when the princess called, Janet had cleared out my desk and hired some new girl.

So I still didn't have a job.

Also, my Blue Sapphire commissions had been returned as part of the deal.

Sam is a little incredulous about my situation. I try to explain it, but it's not easy to describe. One girl. Four guys. All happy.

"Girl, you went poly on me?" she asks.

"I guess you could call it that," I say. "It was an

accident! It just happened."

She laughs. "Only you, Vivienne, could find yourself in an accidental harem."

Huh. Accidental harem.

I like the sound of that.

She promises to wipe my computer of any incriminating data.

But I'm still jobless and rent was due while I was gone. Carrie and Emerald have probably already thrown my stuff out on the street. I never let them know I got stuck on a cruise.

Great. Jobless. Homeless. Poor.

I don't tell the boys any of this. I let them do their business while I lie in the giant bed in the master suite, looking at sunlight and feeling sorry for myself.

That night at dinner, the boys present the plan. Brady and John are going to be based out of Monte Carlo, as Adolfo can shelter their earnings and Mitch would make sure they had rooms in his new place. They would travel, but come back to visit.

Mitch would split his time between Miami and Monte Carlo.

Adolfo would return to Monte Carlo as before.

But what, they ask, do I want to do?

I couldn't say, "Curl up in a ball and die."

"We assumed you'd want to stay near Nashville

to audition," Mitch says.

I cover my head with a pillow. "No point," I say, my voice all muffled.

"You can't give up on your dream," Brady says.

"It's a stupid dream," I say.

"Here's what I suggest," Adolfo says. "You come to Monte Carlo. You can stay with me while Mitch arranges for a new office and residence. Sing in one of the bars. As you earn money, you can fly back to wherever there are auditions. If something works out and you need to be in the states, you can move back to Miami with Mitch or have your own place near the record label."

I move aside the pillow. "Really?"

"It's a good plan," Mitch says. "You still have your own money and your own terms. If you want to throw over any of us, you can do whatever you want."

"But we are here to help," Adolfo says.

"I can put your name out there to open for some of the rodeo acts," Brady says.

"I can't do shit for your career," John says. "But I will fuck the hell out of you during my time off."

I toss the pillow at him.

"How about it?" Mitch says, holding out his hand. "Does it sound good to you?"

I take it and he pulls me to sit up in the middle of

all of them.

"It does," I say. "It's the perfect plan."

Epilogue: Vivienne

The lights brighten the red sequins on my dress as I walk out on stage. It's my lucky dress, the one the boys bought for me on the cruise. I don't wear it often anymore, but today is one year since that fateful mistake, and I'm feeling nostalgic.

The table in the front is full. Brady's here, since the rodeo circuit won't start for another month. Mitch is here, since the weather has been dreadful in Miami anyway. And of course Adolfo has his usual seat. He hasn't missed a show since I started.

John's gone, of course. He can't tell us where he is, but he's loving his assignment and it involves "blowing shit up." When he has breaks, generally I fly to him and get him alone, since it's so rare. The others come in ones and twos and sometimes all three. I call the shots.

So far, it's working. Here in Monte Carlo, I'm a bit of a legend. In a place where big important men have two or three women hanging on them, I'm a novelty. It's inspired a few other ladies to bring their own little harems around. I sometimes seem them after the show, these powerful women and their happy, well-pleased men.

Nobody's judging us here.

The music starts, and I feel good about this song. It's a new one I've been working on for the last month. I finally got the confidence to bring it to the show. I look out over the room. I moved up from the smallest twenty-table cabaret to this stage last summer. It seats about two hundred.

Adolfo had nothing to do with it. I earned my spot with the manager Isabelle, who says she was getting too many requests for my show to leave me in the small theater.

I sing the first words to my favorite table. Mitch, Brady, and Adolfo watch with rapt attention.

Only a foolish heart believes
In only one love
Sometimes it takes losin' and dyin' and cryin'
To find who will put you above

All the others

The music soars and I come around to my favorite part.

I did plenty of that
But now there is you
It's you…you…you…you —

I hold out the note and the perfect acoustics make it resonate through the room. I look at the boys and see them smile, recognizing that I've made the perfect chorus. It can be for one man.

Or for four.

When the last note dies, the applause is tremendous. I look at my table and see all three men looking behind them.

There's a couple seated back there. Their table is marked reserved. I peer at it but can't read who they are from the stage. Maybe somebody famous. I have met a few well-known singers and actors since moving to Monte Carlo.

I bow and walk down the steps. Adolfo kisses my cheek and Brady pulls me into a tight hug.

"Amazing as always, Viv," he says.

I turn to the table they were staring at, now that

I'm closer.

The man and woman are still there, talking quietly and nodding.

I peer at the card. And when I read it, I know what these guys have done. It's right there on the sign.

"Reserved for Gold Discography Records."

I look up at Adolfo. "You didn't," I say.

"I didn't do anything special," he says. "Just an invitation for a lovely couple I met this afternoon. Nothing else. If anything happens, it's all you."

A few members of the audience approach, and I greet them as I always do, taking pictures and accepting their kind words.

As the room starts to clear, I see the two of them are still sitting at their table. Then they stand up and walk toward us.

"Oh my God," I say. "They're coming."

"Be confident," Mitch says. "This is your moment."

The man holds out his hand and I shake it. "Vivienne Carter," he says. "Lovely performance. Do you have an agent?"

Both Adolfo and Mitch speak at the same time, "She does."

The man laughs. "I hope you're not already tied up with some record company. Because I definitely liked what I heard. Was that an original?"

"Yes," I say.

"She has lots more," Brady asks. "A whole record full."

Mitch glares at him to shut up, but the man laughs again. I like him. Despite the fact that his company broke my heart a year ago with the audition I didn't make, he seems nice.

"Well, I'm Phil Barker with Gold Discography. This is my wife June. Do you have some time to chat?"

"I do," I say. "There's a quiet bar on the second floor. Would you two like to come?"

His wife speaks up. "I'm going to go gamble." She looks at Adolfo. "I'm guessing you can teach me how?"

Adolfo holds out his arm. "I would be delighted."

"I'll catch up with you in a bit," Phil says. "I think Vivienne and I have a lot to talk about."

Mitch and Brady stay behind as Phil and I wander through the tables to the upstairs bar. Adolfo and June head to the casino floor.

I glance behind as we leave the room.

Mitch gives me a quick nod, looking pleased. Brady gives me two hearty thumbs up.

I'm grateful for my little band of supporters, the

men who lift me up. I might have come by them accidentally, and never dreamed all five of us would hold together, but we have.

And now, just maybe, my biggest dream is about to come true.

Also by JJ Knight

The UNCAGED LOVE Series
The FIGHT FOR HER Series
SINGLE DAD ON TOP
SINGLE DAD PLUS ONE

www.jjknight.com